THE SEVEN KEYS

JOHN HART

THE SEVEN KEYS

JOHN HART

Published in 1993 by S.P.A.

British Library Cataloguing in Publication Data

A catalogue record for this book is available
from the British Library

ISBN 1 85421 231 1

Designed and Produced by Images Publishing (Malvern) Ltd.
Printed and Bound in Great Britain.

For my grandchildren. Their likes and dislikes, ups and downs, are all reflected in the characters and adventures within these pages.

HOME WORLD

Around Jeremy and Charlotte's house there was a beautiful garden. In it was a magic fountain. A long time ago, the Ancient Sorceress had put the fountain there. She explained that it was called the Fountain of Happiness, because the fountain brought happiness and contentment to all the world. The Sorceress gave Jeremy and Charlotte's parents the secret words that guarded the fountain, and they were the only people who knew the words.

The garden was full of flowers and birds. It was always warm with sunshine, but cooled by the wonderful Fountain of Happiness. The children played in the garden while their parents watched over them. There seemed to be nothing bad or evil that could harm them, nothing that could bring them pain.

Alas, unknown to them, in a world of black spells and dark magic there lived the wicked Evil Wizard. He saw them playing by the Fountain of Happiness and became very jealous of their happiness. He was determined to steal the fountain for his own use. He knew that, by using his blackest spells, he could change it into a fountain of misery. He could then let the waters fall like rain over every land, so that in each town and village no one would be happy any more.

One dark night he came with an army of imps and goblins to steal the fountain. But, to his great fury, he found that the power of the fountain made it impossible to move, unless the children's parents spoke the magic words. Knowing the Evil Wizard's terrible plans they would not speak those words.

The Wizard seized them in a web of enchantment and imprisoned them in his deepest dungeon, behind seven giant doors, each with its own magic key. He then scattered the keys through seven strange and mysterious worlds, saying, "Let someone find these keys and open the doors. Only then the prisoners will go free." He roared with mad laughter, for he knew such a task was impossible.

The old forester, who helped tend the garden, took pity on the lonely children. For a long time Jeremy and Charlotte lived with him in his little wooden cottage in the middle of the forest. Every day and every night, they wished their parents would come back.

One bed time, their old friend told them the story of the Fountain of Happiness. When he finished he said, "The time has come for you to go and rescue your parents from the Wizard's castle." He then explained about the seven keys and the seven doors and how Jeremy and Charlotte would have to cross, the seven worlds.

"There'll be many dangers along the way," he continued, "but you can be sure that a true friend will always be by your side."

Next morning Jeremy and Charlotte got up very early. The cottage was empty, with no trace of the forester. On the table was an old, brown haversack. Inside were just a few oddments: some food, a small mirror and a black cloak. Beside the haversack was a piece of paper, and on it was written "Good Luck."

Then the first of many strange things happened. As Charlotte and Jeremy read the note, it faded away and disappeared, and from behind their backs they heard a faint noise. Quickly they turned round, and there, sitting on the mat was a large black cat, with gold-green eyes.

"Meow," the cat said. "I'm Twitch. What are your names?"

The children were so surprised that they could not speak. But Charlotte finally recovered enough to reply, "I'm Charlotte and that's my brother Jeremy."

"I've never heard a cat talk before," Jeremy said.

The cat stood up and looked around the room. "Sometimes I talk," he half purred, "but, on the other hand, sometimes I don't. It all depends how I feel." He walked over and sniffed at the haversack, touching the cloak with one paw, while he looked at himself in the mirror. "It's a good start," he said, "to have a mirror of magic, and a cloak of invisibility. Better than nothing. Come on then, it's time for us to go."

To the children's surprise, Twitch stalked out of the door and down the path, with his tail stuck straight up in the air. Without a further thought, Charlotte and Jeremy jumped to their feet, lifted the haversack from the table and followed their new friend down the little stony path and through the garden gate. Ahead, the pathway led directly towards the dark forest.

Halfway down the path Charlotte turned around for one last look at the little cottage. As she did so, she could not keep back a cry of amazement which caused Jeremy to stop also and turn.

"The magic's started. The cottage, the pathway behind us, the gate. . . Look, they've disappeared. Look, there's nothing but an empty circle of grass in the middle of the forest."

An impatient voice called out, "Oh do come on, you two, there's a lot to be done."

Jeremy and Charlotte turned and saw Twitch standing, waiting, with the tip of his tail waving slowly.

"We must get through the forest before nightfall," he continued, and without further comment, he plunged into the cold shadows of the giant trees.

On and on they tramped, through the damp, gloomy coldness. Many times the children jumped with fright at strange noises, and many times they thought they saw sharp eyes peering through the bushes or from behind mossy rocks. But every time they turned to look, there was nothing there.

As they became used to the forest, their courage returned. Just when they were beginning to feel quite pleased with themselves, a strange noise filled their ears. Faint at first, but rapidly becoming louder, it was a wailing, screeching sound that hurt their ears and made their heads ring. Then, through patches in the trees they could see a dozen dark shapes, rushing through the air. The shapes became creatures with black cloaks, black tall hats, great hooked noses and claw-like fingers.

"Witches!" said Charlotte, and Jeremy sat down with a bump in fright.

"Don't worry," said Twitch. "They can't get at us through the trees. It's the trolls you need to be careful about. They live in caves in these rocks and are the witches' friends."

Charlotte looked ahead. There was only one path through the thick trees, and it led towards a huge hill of tumbled, jagged rocks.

"But we have to go through those rocks, Twitch," she cried. "What shall we do?"

Twitch looked at her thoughtfully. "Sorry, that's your problem," he said to both of them. "You'll have to learn to look after yourselves if you hope to collect all of the seven keys. I'm sure you'll think of something if we are attacked."

By now they were all very close to the great tumbled heaps of rocks and they could hear the noise of roaring, rushing water. As they turned a bend they saw a fearsome, wide, dark river, dashing swiftly across the pathway ahead. It foamed and crashed against the rocky walls. Swimming in the black waters were countless strange creatures of all shapes and sizes, many with great jaws, filled with pointed teeth. Their red, shining eyes fastened hungrily upon the children.

A flimsy bridge stretched over the frightful waters. It was made of thin silvery strands like spider's webs. The children stopped, horrified at the thought of daring to walk on such a frail support.

It was then that the trolls attacked. Screaming and shouting they poured out from the rocks in their hundreds. They snarled and screeched, their long green hair twisting around their heads like snakes. Their bony fingers, with long black nails, lifted in the air to strike and scratch. From their toothless, slit-like mouths came a screeching whine, and their muddy eyes glared hatefully at Jeremy and Charlotte.

Twitch arched his back and spat, then jumped into Jeremy's arms and hid inside his coat.

Charlotte stepped forward shaking her fist. "Go away, you horrible things!" she shouted. "Go away! Shoo!"

At first, the trolls were amazed and moved back a step or two, for Charlotte really looked so furious. But then a bigger and uglier troll jumped down from a huge rock, its eyes rolling and its mouth wide open. It growled something to the other trolls, who once more started to move towards the children.

"It must be their leader," wailed Jeremy. "We'll never get away."

Then Charlotte thought of the haversack, and she reached inside. Just as the trolls rushed forward, her fingers found the magic mirror. Quickly she held it high above her head. A great flash sprang from it, lighting up the rocky path with an incredible brilliance. The troll leader, as he rushed at the children, was completely dazzled. Unable to see where he was going, he stumbled and fell, rolling down the steep river bank into the waters below. At once the waiting river creatures attacked. The waters foamed and boiled as the evil troll was torn into a thousand pieces. A deafening roar of rage arose from the other trolls when they saw what had happened.

Seizing their chance, the children dashed towards the flimsy bridge, Twitch still hiding in Jeremy's coat. As they set foot on the bridge and started to cross, it swayed and shook. The thin strands which held it up seemed close to breaking. Charlotte glanced back over her shoulder. She saw that the trolls too were starting to cross the bridge, moving with bounding leaps, and quickly catching up.

The children were past the middle. Then they were three quarters of the way across. Charlotte looked down into the shadowy waters and trembled with fear. The trolls were only a few feet behind. One last bound and they would be able to fasten their long fingers on the children's shoulders.

Jeremy cried out in terror. Then Twitch suddenly made up his mind. With a furious "Meow!" he leaped from the cloak and down to the ground right in front of the trolls, spitting and snarling in bristling fury. From the tips of the troll's fingers, spells like balls of blue fire exploded against Twitch's fur, sizzling and smoking dreadfully. But Twitch did not move. For a moment the trolls hesitated, giving the children just enough time to dash across the last few yards and onto firm ground again. At that very moment the spider-web ropes began to snap. The children watched in horror.

"Twitch, Twitch, jump now!" shouted Charlotte.

Twitch gave a backwards leap that landed him safely in Charlotte's arms. As he did so, the ropes finally gave way, and the bridge, together with all the trolls, hurtled down into the ferocious jaws of the waiting river creatures. For a few minutes the waters thrashed and foamed and turned green from the blood of the evil trolls.

By now it was getting dark. Against their wishes, the children had to find a resting place for the night, deep within the blackness of the forest. They made themselves a shelter by throwing their coats over some low branches.

Although they were very tired, they found it hard to sleep, surrounded by the cold, frightening trees. They could still hear weird noises, and could dimly see strange flying shapes. At last, with Twitch snuggling close and warming them with his thick fur, they found their eyes closing.

When they opened their eyes again it was morning. Jeremy sat up first, yawning and stretching his arms and legs which were stiff and aching from the hard ground. The day was grey and misty. The children started to eat their breakfast. There was very little food in the haversack, only a few slices of bread. Twitch ate the crusts, which he seemed to enjoy a great deal.

"Good," whispered Jeremy. "I don't like crusts."

Then, a small noise in the branches over Charlotte's head, made her look up in alarm, but quickly a smile spread over her face. "Look, Jeremy" she said, pointing, and Jeremy turned his head to see. There were two small golden birds sitting on the branches. The birds chirruped to each other, and then, to the children's great surprise, they spoke.

"Please, can you spare us some of your breakfast?" one of the birds said. "It's so dark and cold here."

"There are no berries on the trees, and we are very hungry," continued the other.

The children looked at each other. There was so little food, hardly enough for themselves, but they just could not refuse the little birds. So, smilingly, they shared what they had left between them.

As they finished the last crumbs, the birds shook their wings and rose into the air. Then they flew to the children: one floated down onto Charlotte's shoulder and the other gently landed on Jeremy's. Again they spoke.

"We are spirits of the forest and we know of your search for the seven keys. We shall try to help you if you are ever in trouble. Take this tiny whistle. It is made from an acorn from the Enchanted Oak. When you really need us, blow softly on the whistle, close your eyes and wish."

The birds rose up into the air together and flew around each other, up and down, faster and faster until they looked like one golden flame. Then they were gone.

Unknown to Jeremy and Charlotte, and deep within the darkness of the forest, the witches had heard how their friends the trolls had been destroyed, and they were mad with rage. They were determined to trap the children and to have their revenge, and so they planned carefully. Huddled under a giant poison-tree, they cackled and screeched with spiteful laughter, as they thought how they would deal with the children, once they were caught.

"We'll eat them alive," screamed one.

"No, we'll put them in the oven," spluttered another.

Then the oldest and ugliest witch spoke in a cracked, harsh voice. "We shall keep them as our slaves," she decided, "and make them work for us forever."

All the other witches jumped and flew round and about on their broomsticks, thinking how clever they were.

There was only one path leading through the trees, and over this path the witches hung a large cage, high up so that it could not easily be seen. If anyone should walk exactly under the cage, it could be dropped in an instance, trapping whoever was underneath. To mark the exact place, the witches put some brown leaves on the path. But, now the witches had to decide who would wait beside the path and pull the rope to make the cage fall. Despite their ugly faces and wicked minds, they were all cowards, and not one of them was brave enough to stay close to wait for the children to be trapped. So, they all began to make excuses.

"Not me," said the first one. "I have to collect some more poison for my midnight spell."

"Not me," said the second one. "I have to visit the Wizard of the Blue Mountains."

Within a few minutes all the witches had invented a reason not to have to wait.

The leader looked around. "I know who will do it," she cackled. "There's one witch who is not here – the old witch of the Cave of Bats. She doesn't know about the children so we won't tell her. She cannot see very well, so she will not see them properly, as they come round the bend. We shall tell her to pull the rope when she hears the dry leaves crackle, and we shall tell her that we are catching a wild rock-beast for our spells."

That's just what they did. With the cage hanging high in the trees,

14

the old witch of the Cave of Bats settled back, waiting, listening and mumbling to herself.

By now the children had put their coats back on and had set off down the path again. But this time the eyes they thought they could see and the noises they thought they could hear were real. Creeping through the bushes were a dozen hungry hobgoblins, with red, stupid-looking faces, and short stumpy legs, and big fat stomachs. They did not look at all dangerous, but they certainly were. If you could have looked closely, you would have seen that the stupid faces had mouths full of large pointed teeth, and their hands and feet had long, tearing claws. All the time they gobbled and licked their lips at the thought of the tasty meal Jeremy and Charlotte would make.

On and on the children walked, and all the time they drew closer to the witches' trap. Meanwhile the hobgoblins were steadily building their courage up to attack.

At last, with a screaming rush they dashed out upon the children, almost at the moment that Jeremy was about to tread, unknowingly, on the dry, brown leaves. Charlotte screamed and pushed Jeremy sideways into the bushes, tumbling head over heels the other way herself. The hobgoblins were rushing so fast that they were unable to stop. They dashed past, onto the leaves.

The old witch heard the noise. With all her strength, she pulled the rope. In front of the children's disbelieving eyes, the great cage fell out of the trees above, landing with a terrible crash. A huge cloud of dust covered the hobgoblins. When the dust settled Jeremy and Charlotte could see that every single hobgoblin was trapped in the cage.

The noise they made was terrible, like a hundred railway engines. They screeched and wailed. The cage shook and rattled as the furious hobgoblins tried to break out. The old witch was alarmed. She could hear the noise and could dimly see that the cage was being roughly shaken although she could not see what was inside.

"The rock-beast is getting loose," she moaned, rocking backwards and forwards in fright. "It's mad with rage. I don't want it to get free, it'll tear me to pieces. Oh dear, oh dear."

There was an even louder scream of rage and such a terrible rattling of the cage that the witch was scared into action. Lifting up her hands she screamed a number of magic words, bringing a swarming cloud of explosion-bees around her head. She pointed her long, brown finger at the cage and whispered a command. With a whirring hum the bees flew straight into the open, ugly mouths of the hobgoblins. As the witch lifted her hand and pointed once more, a faint, green light flickered from her finger towards the cage and the bees exploded in a blinding flash of purple lightening.

Jeremy and Charlotte fell backwards into the prickly bushes, quite unable to believe their eyes. Where a moment ago there had been an enormous cage, full of spiteful, wicked hobgoblins, now all that was left was a bare smoking patch on the path, together with some more green blood splattered on nearby trees and a few burnt ropes dangling from the tree above.

By now the children and Twitch were in a real panic. Pulling themselves out from the bushes, they rushed along the path, tripping over brambles, and bumping into trees. At last they had to stop, for they were completely out of breath.

"That was quite unnecessary," Twitch gasped. "The hobgoblins are gone. Surely there's nothing to fear in the forest now. In any case, we must be nearly out of the trees and then it's going to be much easier."

The children set off once more along the path. Twitch was proven right: around the next bend the trees began to thin, and the air grew brighter. Finally, the forest was behind them, and they found themselves on a wide plain of green grass which stretched away as far as the eye could see.

All day long the children tramped across the grass under a grey, sunless sky. They had no idea whether or not they were going the right way, as all directions looked the same. However, Twitch seemed to know which way to take, and marched on in front of them with his tail sticking straight up like a flag-pole. The children followed him, on and on. In the middle of the afternoon, Charlotte

17

stopped and said, "Oh, Twitch, we really must have a rest. I'm tired out."

Jeremy was glad. He was exhausted, but he didn't want to say anything in case the others made fun of him.

They all lay back on the soft grass. They were almost asleep when Twitch sprang to his feet, spitting and screeching, his fur and whiskers standing on end. Charlotte sat up in fright, and what she saw made her cry out to Jeremy at the top of her voice.

"Wake up, wake up!" she screamed. "We are being attacked!"

Jeremy jumped to his feet and ran to Charlotte's side. The air was full of noise and movement. Screams and mad laughter filled his ears as he saw ten or more witches diving and flapping, wheeling and turning in the air overhead. Jeremy and Charlotte looked around for somewhere to hide. There was nowhere. And they had no weapons to fight with.

The witches looked full of mad rage and fury. From their pointed fingers they threw spells of red and blue fire which exploded into flames around the children. From the witches' black cloaks grey smoke puffed and floated with a smell like bad eggs, so bad that the smallest whiff made the children sick with disgust.

The spells were clustering closer and closer, and the horrible smoke was getting thicker. Although she knew that they had to try to escape, Charlotte found herself almost unable to move, until suddenly she felt a sharp pain in her hand which made her jump. She looked down and saw Twitch watching her worriedly.

"Sorry I had to stick my claws in your hand," he said, "but I had to do something to get you to listen to me."

"Sssssssss!" A ball of fire sizzled a few centimetres away. "'Boooomph!" Another landed just behind her. Charlotte cried out in alarm, "Do you have any idea what we can do, Twitch?"

Twitch nodded. "The cloak. Get it out of the haversack. Under it we'll be invisible to the witches, and they will not know where to throw their spells."

Charlotte hunted through the haversack. Taking the cloak, she threw it over hers and Jeremy's shoulders. It was only just large enough to cover them both and so Twitch had to sit across their feet. "Keep absolutely still," Charlotte ordered, "if we make any move at

18

all, the cloak will slip from over us and the witches will spot us," so they sat very, very, still, waiting to see what would happen.

"They've gone!" one of the witches cried out. "They've disappeared!"

Through a little gap Jeremy could see the witches' ugly red eyes glaring and flaming and their green teeth snapping as they whirled around and around. Jeremy, Charlotte and Twitch sat and trembled with fright at the noise.

All of a sudden Twitch started to sing. He was really more used to wailing on roof-tops at night than singing, and his voice was absolutely awful. In fact, it was so dreadful that Jeremy and Charlotte began to laugh. They made sure the cloak still covered them, but now they could all see the witches.

The wicked creatures heard the laughter and looked this way and that, up and down. Everywhere. But, of course, they could not see where it was coming from. So they became wilder and wilder and madder still as they twisted around, spinning across the sky faster and faster, flying up and down at terrible, dangerous speeds.

At last, with an ear shattering bang, two of them collided. A huge black and orange ball of fire spread around them. In the middle of the fire, the bottles of wicked, evil spells started to explode: spells that would turn you into a frog, or a snake, or a bat. One huge bottle broke into a hundred pieces, letting loose a thick, green smoke that made everything it touched shrink. The exploding bottles filled the air with escaped spells. The witches, flying around so fast, could not dodge them. Within seconds they were in the middle of all the dreadful magic.

Suddenly, all was quiet. At first, Charlotte and Jeremy could not understand what had happened. They pulled down the cloak from over their heads and looked all around. The grassy floor was covered with frogs hopping and snakes slithering, whilst above them, dozens of bats flapped away into the distance. There were even a few tiny witches scurrying around, but in no time at all these were caught and swallowed by the frogs. It was the end of all the witches and their terrible spells. Soon, every frog, snake and bat had gone too. The children and Twitch were alone on the wide grassy plain.

Jeremy, Charlotte and Twitch started walking in single file along the path again. It led straight through the level grass. Gradually it started to climb until the children found themselves on the top of a low hill.

As they started climbing down again the scenery changed. There were thick bushes on both sides of the path. Halfway across the valley, the path continued underneath the low branches of an immense tree, and each branch was covered with long, sharp hooks. On the very top of the tree there was a wide, red opening which seemed to move and change size the whole time.

"What on earth is it?" wondered Jeremy out loud, but neither Charlotte nor Twitch could answer.

As they stood watching, something happened. A strange little creature started to hop along the path. It looked like a pig, with thin, long legs and a purple frill down its back. It was chewing at the grass as it moved slowly. Hop, hop, hop. Along the pathway, nearer and nearer to the tree it moved until exactly under the lowest branches. Then something strange happened to the tree: it seemed to shake a little and quiver all the way down. Suddenly, the branches thrashed down, instantly trapping the animal in their hooks.

There was no escape. The branches lifted into the air, up towards the red opening which had now stretched to twice its size. For a moment the animal was held high over the opening. With a quick movement, the branches released the creature and it fell directly down into the red opening.

"It's the tree's mouth!" Jeremy exclaimed.

"That's no ordinary tree," said Charlotte. "If it eats animals, it'll probably eat us too."

Jeremy and Charlotte looked around. The bushes were so close and thick that there was only the one way to go: straight under the tree.

They stood on the path, not knowing what to do, until Charlotte, staring at the terrible tree, half sobbed,

Oh Jeremy, it looks like we have to give up our search almost before it's started . . ."

Then as she started to turn round, there was a terrible noise.

Not a hundred yards away the children saw, to their shocked

surprise, a band of two-headed ogres rushing and tumbling towards them.

"It's them!" one of the creatures shouted. "They destroyed our friends!"

"Let's catch them and take them away," shouted another. "We'll fatten them up and eat them at the next full moon."

Charlotte and Jeremy knew that it would be of no use to try to hide under the Cloak of Invisibility again. They could not run anywhere to escape because of the killer tree.

But it was Twitch who, once again, came to the rescue. He wasn't in a talking mood, but he pointed to the haversack.

"Of course," Charlotte said, scrambling to open it. "The whistle! Oh why don't I think of these things myself?"

She snatched the whistle from the haversack as fast as she could and, lifting it to her lips, she closed her eyes and blew softly. Strangely, there was no noise, but the whistle grew warmer and warmer until it became so hot she could no longer hold it. With a cry of surprise Charlotte let it fall to the ground.

Amazingly, the little acorn-whistle began to grow in size. In an instance it became a large, shiny bubble with a small door in the side.

"Jump in!" said Twitch. "There's no time to lose."

Jeremy, Charlotte and Twitch jumped through the door, slamming it shut at the very moment that the ogre's fingers were reaching out to seize them.

The ogres crashed and hammered on the bubble from every side. The noise was terrifying. Jeremy and Charlotte felt sure that their flimsy protection would soon break. But despite every effort, the enraged ogres were unable to make even a small dent in the shiny walls. The children could see the angry faces of the ogres pressed against the glassy round window, but they felt safe.

Suddenly, the silvery bubble floated into the air, carrying the three along the pathway towards the terrible tree. As it drew nearer, the children became quiet. Twitch licked their fingers and purred at them as if to say "Don't worry."

In a few minutes they were directly under the low-hanging hooks of the branches. The tree lashed and whipped at the bubble, but even with its gigantic strength it made no impression, and the bubble floated quietly onwards along the path.

"We're safe," said Jeremy.

"Wait!" said Charlotte. "I don't think the ogres have given up yet."

The ogres hurled themselves after the bubble. But, too late they saw the menace of the great tree, and in the sheer speed and madness of their attack, they were unable to stop. In a flash the thorny branches slashed down, scooped up the evil creatures, lifted them and dropped them down into the wide-open quivering mouth.

The bubble landed softly in the middle of a wide meadow. After Jeremy, Charlotte and Twitch stepped out they heard a tuneful "Pop" and the bubble disappeared.

The children turned their heads just in time to see the last of the ogres fall into the tree-mouth. Jeremy was in the middle of saying "That's the end of them," when a great tremble shook the whole great tree from one end to the other. The shaking and thrashing of the branches became more and more violent. Brown leaves and thousands of the long sharp thorns fell like rain.

"It's the ogres' poison," Twitch explained.

The air was filled with a shrill, grating noise, growing louder every second. With a deafening crash, the entire tree exploded into a heap of smoking, brown dust, which was swiftly and silently blown away by the breeze.

For a while there was the deepest silence the children had ever known. It was as time stood still. Not a murmur of the breeze could be heard, nor the slightest rustle of the grass and not a bird sang.

The children waited, not daring to speak. Something terribly important was about to happen, they were sure. As they waited, there was a great flash of golden light, which for a moment dazzled them so they were unable to see. They screwed up their eyes tightly.

As Charlotte and Jeremy opened their eyes again, they gasped in wonder. Gone were the grey skies and heavy clouds. Gone was the frightening, dark forest and the thick thorny bushes. All around, as far as the eye could see was soft, green grass under a blue sky. The sun shone, and the warm air was filled with the scent of the thousands of flowers of every colour which popped their heads out between the soft blades of grass.

Quite exhausted by all that had happened, the children dropped to the ground, closed their eyes and stretched out in the warm sunshine. They didn't notice that they were being surrounded by rabbits, squirrels, field-mice, birds of all colours and other little animals.

Jeremy was the first one to open his eyes. "Look, Charlotte!" he exclaimed.

In front of all the little animals were the two golden birds. Flying close to the children, the first one said, "You three have been very brave. You've helped to destroy the spirits of wickedness and terror which the Wizard put here in revenge, when he found that he could not take the Fountain of Happiness. Now we can all live happily and safely again."

"Take this," said the other bird. "It is your reward for everything you've done for us."

"Thank you," Charlotte and Jeremy said together.

"Maybe we'll see you back with us one day," the birds said, and they rose into the air. As before, they shone and sparkled as they wheeled and spun around faster and faster, like shining golden balls until, suddenly, they were gone.

On the grass was a small box. As Charlotte took it in her hand she saw that it was made from rabbit's down curiously woven with tiny goose feathers.

"Open it," said Jeremy.

Charlotte lifted the lid. "Oh!" she gasped. She held the box out for Jeremy and Twitch to see for themselves.

They too were speechless when they saw what was inside: a small, golden key.

The first one . . .

ICE WORLD

The warm, gentle breezes and the songs of the birds began to make the children very sleepy. The many dangers they had met had made them so tired, that soon their eyes began to close. With their new friends all around them, they were soon fast asleep. They curled up on the soft grass with Twitch stretched out between them.

They slept for a long time, long enough for them to recover their strength. But perhaps they would have slept even longer, had they not been woken up by a feeling of intense cold. Charlotte sat up shivering. With her teeth chattering, she pulled her coat tighter around her shoulders.

"Why is it so cold?" she asked.

Jeremy was by now also awake and shivering. "What's happened?" he said. "I'm freezing."

"I'm frozen too!" said Charlotte. "It seems really odd that the weather has changed so quickly. I thought that the golden birds said this world would now always be sunny and warm since the bad spirits had gone."

Twitch was sitting upright, his feet tucked under his tail. He turned his green-gold eyes towards Charlotte and said, "The birds did tell you that, but that was on Home World. Look around, things are different now."

Jeremy and Charlotte peered through the darkness. They could just see that they were in a small hollow, sheltered by trees. When they looked through the branches all they could see was a great expanse of ice and snow, bare and empty. A cold wind moaned through the trees, sending up small flurries of the powdery snow here and there.

"I can't believe it," Charlotte said.

"It's the next world," Jeremy said. "We have the first key and now, somehow, we've been taken to a new world to find the second key."

"You're right," said Charlotte. "The keys must be joined by the same magic."

"Yes," Jeremy continued. "I think that when we find one of them, its enchanted spell draws us to where the next key is hidden."

Charlotte nodded thoughtfully. Jeremy was most probably right, and so they had to get moving without further delay. She stepped forward, outside the shelter of the trees, and now the full force of the wind hit her, making her shiver even more.

Twitch looked really miserable. Shaking inside his fur, he scrambled up inside Jeremy's cloak and snuggled close, with just his whiskers poking out.

In the distance there was a low line of hills, under grey skies, full of heavy, dark clouds. From the clouds large snow-flakes began to fall, silently settling on the children and quickly making them look like walking snowmen.

A weak feeling began to spread though Charlotte and she knew she must do something fast before the coldness froze the life out of them.

"The haversack!" The thought flashed through her mind. Immediately, she undid the straps and looked at the things inside. Was there anything that might help? They didn't need the Cloak of Invisibility: it is not possible to hide from the cold. Perhaps the magic acorn-whistle? No. That was surely for protection against evil creatures. The mirror? Of course! It was a magic mirror and could therefore help in all kinds of ways. It must surely help against the terrible cold? Charlotte took the mirror from the haversack. The silvery surface reflected a swirl of colours that constantly shifted and moved. Gazing deeply into them Charlotte whispered, "Please help us, Mirror. We are so cold."

A small fire seemed to glow within the depths of the mirror. With a cry of surprise Charlotte dropped it onto the soft snow. The fire flickered and grew.

"Quick!" Charlotte said. "Let's gather some twigs."

Jeremy and Charlotte piled twigs and small branches over the flames. Soon the fire was blazing high, melting the snow from their clothes and warming them through and through.

"I feel better now," said Jeremy.

"Yes, now I feel strong enough to set off again," said Charlotte. But as she stood up she thought of the magic mirror now buried under the bonfire.

"Poor mirror," she said to Jeremy.

"Look," Jeremy said, pointing at the open haversack.

Charlotte saw a faint gleam inside. To her amazement, there was the mirror safely tucked away beside the Cloak of Invisibility.

With the haversack safely on her shoulders, Charlotte looked around again. Far away on the top of the hills, a light was burning, bright and clear through the falling snow.

"Come on," Charlotte said.

"Let's go," Jeremy agreed. "We have to reach that light."

As they stepped out onto the wide, snowy plain, the wind began to slacken and the snow stopped falling. They started to march directly across the great white expanse, towards the far distant light.

They talked about Home World and their adventures. They were so engrossed in their talking, that they did not notice the strange faces that flickered from behind the trees. Neither did they hear the shrill, whistle like voices that floated through the darkness.

They were unaware that a pack of ice-demons hiding in the snowy shadows were following their every move. These dreadful creatures roamed the whole land, bringing dread to everyone. On the darkest nights they raided the little houses of the snow-people, carrying away many captives, some to eat and some to keep forever as their slaves.

Jeremy was a little ahead as the children climbed up a small hillock, so it was he who first saw the row of tiny houses, only three feet tall, half buried in the snow. As Charlotte joined him and they stood staring in surprise, a crowd of little people ran forward to meet them.

"Look at their legs," Charlotte whispered. Their arms and legs were green, their hair was white and their little faces glowed bright red.

"They look like walking Christmas trees," Jeremy whispered back.

The little creatures were very excited at seeing the children and they danced around them, chattering in deep voices. They beckoned to Jeremy and Charlotte, inviting the children into their tiny homes.

26

Crouching down, Charlotte and Jeremy just managed to crawl through the tiny door. Once inside they were very cramped, barely able to sit. Even with their knees drawn up, their heads were touching the ceiling. To add to their discomfort, the light was so dim and the air so full of smoke from the fire, that at first they could scarcely see across the narrow room.

One of the snow-people threw some more wood on the fire and, as the flames danced upwards, the room became brighter. The children were able to see that the small room was absolutely crowded.

"That's strange," Charlotte whispered, "the house looked so small from the outside, and yet, inside, it's big enough to hold everyone!"

She was right. There seemed to be hundreds of the little people packed into the one room of the house, and all of them were gazing at Jeremy and Charlotte from bright, twinkling eyes.

"Tell us about your adventures," one of the little snow-people said.

Jeremy and Charlotte looked at each other.

"You start," Jeremy said.

Charlotte looked at the snow-people and started. For quite some time Charlotte and then Jeremy told of their adventures and their hunt for the keys.

"You will find many dangers here," the same little snow-person said in a serious voice. As he turned towards the children the room became quiet, and all the little faces ceased to smile but became sad and anxious. "There are many dangers now."

"Now?" Charlotte asked.

"Yes. This world used to be sunny and bright with not one evil thing upon it. There was no snow or ice and we slept out in the open under the stars. Then one day a young girl, happily playing with her ball, accidentally threw it through the open window of the Evil Wizard's castle. It landed with a great splash in the cauldron of magic that was bubbling over the open fire. The splashes flew around, and the magic boiled over, onto the ground. Many spells were lost, and some of them turned into strange creatures. In his temper, the Wizard let the creatures loose upon this land." The little snow-person paused.

27

"And what are these creatures?" Jeremy asked.

"There are ice demons, cloud ghosties, devil lights, crystal bats and rock creepers. Most of them are wicked and horrible. The wizard was so full of rage at losing his spells that, as well as letting loose these creatures, he sent the snow clouds and the ice storms. And now we can never go far because of the dangers, and the terrible cold, and none of our children can play outside as they used to a long time ago."

Everyone was silent. No one seemed to have anything more to say. Jeremy and Charlotte were just getting ready to move when one of the other snow-people spoke:

"Only someone who is good and brave can defeat these monsters and reach the everlasting Fire of Achievement that burns forever on the top of the silver mountains. Then the spells will be broken, and the world will be happy again."

As if on an invisible signal, the snow-people rose to their feet and quietly filed out of the little door, leaving only the one who had first spoken. He seemed to be older than the others, though it was difficult to tell, as they all looked so small. His hair and his long beard were streaked with silver. The children realised he must be the leader.

"We must get to the Fire of Achievement to save you," Jeremy said.

"Yes, we'll get there," agreed Charlotte.

"Take these things," the snow-person said, pointing to some objects which lay upon the floor. "They will help you along the way." He held out a small crystal bottle. "This contains Water of Protection. Scatter it when you are in danger." Then he lifted up two beautiful cloaks. "These are made of woven moonbeams and will keep out the cold." Finally he said, "This little box contains food, and this flask is filled to the brim with soup. Neither the box, nor the flask will ever empty."

"Thank you," said both Charlotte and Jeremy.

He waved his hands gently in front of the children, "Now sleep," he said. "You'll need all your strength tomorrow." Then he left.

"I've a feeling that we'll find the second key in the Silver Mountains," Charlotte whispered to Jeremy as they both lay down on the soft, warm floor.

"So have I," said Jeremy.

They closed their eyes, and in a second they were sound asleep. Twitch curled up between the children and was soon fast asleep too.

The next morning, the snow-people had all gone. The little houses were empty and the streets deserted and silent. The cold seemed to be more bitter than ever. The children were reluctant to move.

Twitch said, "Come on, we really must get a move on. Anyway, I'm hungry!"

Jeremy opened the flask of soup, finding that the lid was, in fact, three small cups that fitted inside one another.

"There's just enough for one helping each," he said as he filled the cups.

But to his absolute amazement, when he looked into the flask, it was still full to the top. It was the same with the little box of food. Inside were only three small sandwiches, and Charlotte could see, quite plainly, when she took them out, that the box was empty, but when she looked back, a moment later, there were three more sandwiches in it.

After their breakfast, they felt strong enough to face the cold outside. Looking across the great stretch of deep snow, they could see the light still brightly burning against the black sky. They set off straight towards it.

All that morning they marched on, in happy spirits, talking and guessing at what they might find when they reached the Fire of Achievement.

They were quite unaware that the ice demons were very close. Having smelt the food they were raving mad with hunger. Their iced mouths, full of sharp teeth hung open. Their leathery tongues licked in and out at the thought of capturing the children. These terrible creatures could leap thirty metres into the air and, hidden by the drifting snow clouds, could easily follow every move the children made. Their long trailing hair was a smoky grey, exactly the colour of the sky, so even when they were within a few yards of the children, they could not be seen.

They trailed along, growing closer and closer to the three travellers. Finally one of them could wait no longer and leapt towards Jeremy.

"Help!" Jeremy cried. He turned quickly, trying to get out of the ice demon's grasp, and when doing so, dropped his moonbeam cloak.

The ice demon breathed out a great cloud of icy breath. Jeremy was frozen into a block of ice. Quick as a flash, Charlotte took the cloak from where it had dropped to the ground and wrapped it warmly around him. As she did so, the ice demon crashed down with a roar like thunder.

The awful creature was so close that Jeremy could see that its hair was made from snow-crystals and its eyes were balls of green ice, and from its twisted mouth roared a hurricane of freezing air. Crouching low, the demon fixed its eyes upon the children. To their horror they found that they were unable to move even a finger. The terrible creature crawled closer and seized hold of Jeremy with one of his huge claws. With a hissing growl, it reached out for Charlotte.

All of a sudden, there was a terribly loud "Meeeeeeooowww!" It sounded as if a bomb had burst. Twitch sprang forward and with one great sweep of his paw he scratched at the demon's icy eye.

Mad with pain and rage, the demon uttered a thunderous roar and lashed out with both huge arms, throwing Twitch through the air.

As the icy breath left her, Charlotte could move again. She reached for the Waters of Protection. As the demon recovered and rushed at her again, she opened the bottle and dashed some of the contents directly into his face.

What happened next was almost unbelievable. Charlotte remained fixed to the spot as the magic water began to work. The water turned into blue fire, spreading and running like paint until it covered the whole of the demon's body. He screeched and screamed as he began to melt away. Jeremy fell to the ground unhurt as the great claws holding him dissolved into water.

With a final thick cloud of rising steam, the ice demon was completely destroyed. All that remained was a small pool of water which soon soaked into the snow.

31

Jeremy and Charlotte looked in amazement as the other demons melted and shrank. With the destruction of their leader, their magic was finished.

"Where's Twitch?" Jeremy asked.

"There he is," said Charlotte, pointing at the cat.

"Pretty good, don't you think?" he purred, as he walked towards them.

The three continued on their journey. Twitch stalked away in front, with his tail twisting and turning in the air.

The flat, white plain stretched on and on, and the silver mountains seemed as far away as when Charlotte and Jeremy had first started. They came to a great heap of tumbled rocks that rose out from the snow. As they came very near the rocks there was suddenly a loud whistling noise, and a huge shower of sparks flew high into the air. The children looked around, in all directions, but they still could not see what had caused it.

"Look," said Jeremy, "if you stand close to the rocks you can't feel the cold wind."

Charlotte tried. "You're right," she said.

"There's a hollow here," continued Jeremy.

"It will be warmer in there." said Charlotte.

From deep within the ground there seemed to be a low throbbing sound, just loud enough to hear. But the children had little time to wonder about this, for in an instance there was a terrible roaring and grinding, the rocks opened beneath their feet and they found themselves falling into a terrifying pit of blackness.

Down and down they fell. As their eyes grew used to the dim light they could see that they were in a steeply sloping passageway which carried them, head over heels, deep into the ground. With a sudden bump they hit the bottom, rolling over and over until they came to a stop against a wall.

The only light was a dull red glow which seemed to be coming from the rocky walls around them, and the children had difficulty in seeing anything, except some weird, moving shapes.

"What's that?" whispered Jeremy.

"I don't know," Charlotte said, still trying to make her eyes get used to the dim light.

The cave was huge, so wide across that the furthest walls were lost in the red shadows. Lined up all around the children were a large number of misshapen creatures, reddish-blue in colour and hard to see against the blackness of the rocks. Their appearance was too ugly for words – a strange mixture of very old, shrivelled men and worn pieces of rock. As they moved they made odd scratching noises. The children shrank back as they saw them approach and their terror increased when they heard them speak.

"We are the rock-creepers," one larger and more shrunken than the rest said, in a low, grinding voice, "and we have always lived deep within these caves. We have never seen creatures like you before, and probably never will do so again. Now you are here, we shall keep you with us forever, to amuse us in the long evenings. There is no way you can escape!"

The rock-creeper then became silent, and for a long time there was no sound at all. The strange creatures stood absolutely still staring at the children, until at last as if on an unspoken signal they turned and filed away, and were lost in the shadows.

Jeremy and Charlotte were so tired that they settled down on the hard floor to try to rest. Their eyes grew heavy. With Twitch lying across their feet they were soon fast asleep.

When they awoke, it was still to the same dim, red light. Immediately Charlotte jumped to her feet and looked anxiously around, but the rock-creepers were nowhere to be seen. Her first thought was that now they could explore and find a way to escape. But as she rose to her feet she found that, whilst they were asleep, both she and Jeremy had been fastened to the rocky walls. They were unable to move more than a metre in any direction.

All day the two children talked and tried to plan a way out, and they both tried, over and over again to unfasten the chains that held them. They found that the locks, although small and light, were immensely strong. No amount of smashing them against the rocks had any effect.

Later, much later, the rock-creepers filed silently back into the great cave. The chains around the children were unfastened, and the two were forced to walk up and down and round about, to the never ending clicks and growls of amusement from the strange creatures. Free from their chains, the children looked for a chance to escape, but they were watched so closely that they soon began to lose all hope.

On the second day Charlotte had an idea. A plan formed in her mind that might help them to get away. She moved over to Jeremy, as quietly as she could, and whispered into his ear.

"Yes, that's it!" Jeremy whispered back as he clapped his hands silently together in delight.

No time was to be lost. The sooner the plan was put into action, the better and so Jeremy immediately started on the first part of it.

"Oh dear! Oh dear!" Jeremy's groans sounded terrible, echoing back from the walls and roof of the huge cave. "Oh dear! Oh dear!" he repeated as he rolled around on the ground kicking hard at the loose stones and rocks, so as to make as much noise as possible.

"Ouch! Help!" Jeremy was certainly putting on quite an act.

Charlotte thought that perhaps he was overdoing it a bit. She was just about to tell him so, when she heard the clicking and scraping of the approaching rock-creepers. The plan was working.

Now it was time for Charlotte to join in. Her screams and moans, her sobs and cries could have been heard for miles. Twitch helped, by meowing as loud as he could. The rock-creepers hurried even faster to see what was happening.

"What's the fuss about?" demanded a creeper in its odd, grating voice.

"We are starving," moaned Charlotte. "We can't live without our food. We have to have it every few hours and we can't last much longer. You must let me get to it or by tonight we'll all be dead."

The creeper looked at them suspiciously. Charlotte had really made herself look ill. Jeremy looked even worse. All his shouting and groaning had made his face turn bright red. When the rock-creeper looked at him he rolled his eyes round and round.

With great caution the creeper unlocked Charlotte's chains and allowed her to open the box of sandwiches. That was all she needed. While she ate, she secretly rubbed the butter from the sandwiches onto her ankles. The moment she finished eating she was once more locked up.

The creeper then unlocked Jeremy who did exactly the same as Charlotte, thoroughly covering his ankles with butter. Soon both children were again securely fastened and they leaned quietly back, waiting for the creeper to go.

They both waited a while until they were sure that the creeper had really gone. Then, tugging and pulling, wriggling and twisting Jeremy managed to slip the thin chains from his feet. He was free! A few moments later and Charlotte was free too. The plan had worked.

Quickly, Charlotte dashed over to Twitch and rubbed butter into his fur to set him free. Then, as planned, Jeremy and Twitch hid behind the rocks while Charlotte settled back to await the rock-creepers' return.

Time seemed to go very slowly. Twitch curled up and went to sleep. Charlotte and Jeremy tried to play some guessing games but they soon felt so bored with the waiting that they began to nod too. Suddenly Charlotte sat up, fully awake. She had heard a faint noise and, straining her ears she listened hard. Yes! She had not imagined it – the rock-creepers were returning.

"Keep absolutely still," she warned the others. "The creepers must not see that we are free until we are ready." She checked to make sure that the bottle containing the Water of Protection was close by her hand. "Remember," she said again, "DO NOT MOVE!"

"Right," said Jeremy.

As the rock-creepers shuffled into the great cave some of the dust in the air got into Jeremy's nose. Before he could do anything to stop himself, he sneezed – not once, not twice, but three times, making him roll over and over on the ground. At once the creatures watching saw that he was no longer chained.

Clustering together, the creepers moved menacingly forwards, very angry to see that the children had somehow freed themselves. As they drew nearer, Charlotte lifted the bottle of Magic Water high in the air.

"Keep away," she warned, "or I'll scatter this over you."

The rock-creepers became amazingly enraged. They jumped and shouted and stamped up and down. Charlotte had such a fit of giggles that she almost dropped the flask. Then, becoming very serious, she again spoke to the creatures.

"Now, let us out immediately, or you'll all be destroyed."

Again the creepers went into the fits of rage that had made Charlotte laugh before, but they soon stopped. They started to lead the children towards a long, twisting stone tunnel.

Charlotte gave a great sigh of relief when, at the far end of the tunnel she saw the sky. Then she turned towards the rock-creepers.

"Now you go back," she shouted in her fiercest voice. "Right back to the far side of the cave."

At first it seemed as though the creatures were too furious at losing their prisoners to obey. But when Charlotte took the top from the bottle and waved it at them they moved off as fast as they could. They were soon gone, lost in the red shadows.

Soon Jeremy, Charlotte and Twitch were running away from the rocks as fast as they could. As they ran they heard the strange whistling noise.

Charlotte turned her head and gasped. "Look!" she said.

There was a brilliant shower of sparks flying into the sky from the rocks behind.

They ran and ran, gasping and panting until they could run no further. Night began to fall and great black clouds began to fill the sky. When they came to a thick clump of bushes ahead, they squeezed underneath, wrapping their moonbeam cloaks around themselves to keep out the freezing cold.

However, neither Jeremy nor Charlotte could get to sleep. The excitement of the past few hours had left them wide awake, and so they talked for a while.

"Tell me about the time before the Wizard took mum and dad away," Jeremy said to Charlotte.

"We used to sit by the Fountain of Happiness with our picnic basket. We played with balls of silver and gold. The sun was always shining. Daddy used to give us piggy-backs and mummy used to read her book, leaning against a mossy bank until the tinkling of the water lulled her to sleep."

Jeremy himself was just nodding off when a faint sound drifted through the darkness. It was a sound like tinkling bells, sometimes soft, but sometimes loud. Both children crawled out from under the bushes and looked up into the night sky, and there they saw a crowd of many coloured lights. There were hundreds of them twisting and turning, spinning and wheeling like a great fireworks display.

Gradually the lights came closer. The children were now able to see that each one was a tiny creature and they were all sparkling in reds, blues, yellows, greens, all colours of the rainbow. Every one was glowing like a small candle. Now the little creatures were so very close that their voices could be heard clearly.

"Do not be afraid. And do not worry."

"Who are you?" asked Charlotte.

"We are called the Cloud Ghosties by the little people who live on this world, and we can always tell bad from good. We know that you are brave and strong, and we can tell you that you will win through in the end."

Twitch was not feeling too happy. The hundreds of lights quite frightened him. The children smiled as he took a sudden leap to hide in the haversack, with just his tail sticking out. Then, when they turned back to the sky, they saw that the Cloud Ghosties were floating away. Soon every trace of them was gone. The few stars that had been showing were now covered once more by the thick black clouds. Everywhere was dark again.

The snow had started to fall heavily. The children felt very tired, so they went back to the shelter of the thick bushes and snuggled down inside their warm cloaks.

The next morning was bright and clear. With the sun warming their backs, Jeremy and Charlotte marched steadily on. They passed several villages of the snow-people, but all the houses were empty, and not one of the little people did they see. Except for the three travellers nothing moved on that great white world of snow.

Towards evening Jeremy and Charlotte could see that they were now much closer to the silver mountains, and the ever-burning flame was now a flare of brilliance against the darkening sky. The children could even see that it came from the top of a great tower, high in the mountains, and they were certain that, the next day, they would be searching for a way up.

All looked calm. The children decided to settle for the night under an enormous oak tree. But Twitch was very restless and just would not settle down. He suddenly jumped up and dashed off across the snow.

He came rushing back in a great panic, making loud "Meows" of fright. The children jumped up and saw half a dozen swooping beings. They were as big as eagles, with enormous beaks full of sharp teeth, and their bodies shone with a million crystal scales. Their feathers rustled and clashed with a glassy ring.

"They are the bats, Jeremy." Charlotte shouted. "You remember what the snow-people said – the crystal bats. They are really evil."

That was all she had time to say. Seeing the children the bats immediately attacked, diving and wheeling, flashing around in circles at tremendous speeds. Jeremy threw his arms up to protect Charlotte just as the great curved claws slashed across towards her face. The razor-sharp claws slashed across his hand, drawing blood, and making him cry out with the sudden pain.

Twitch seized the haversack in his mouth and dragged it across to Charlotte. Reaching behind her, she grasped the first thing her fingers touched: the magic mirror. She held it before her as the Bats came in to attack her again. Such was the force of the evil creatures, that the mirror was almost torn from her grasp. She managed to hold on to it and as the shining face of the mirror was tilted slightly towards her, she saw a spot of light beginning to glimmer and grow. Quickly she turned the mirror back towards the crowding bats. A blue light flashed from the mirror with such a fierce brightness, that the children could hardly bear to look.

As the light touched the bats, they shattered into a million pieces of ice, with a deafening ringing noise. The blue ray was so powerful that even the bats the furthest away, were caught in its powerful magic and were also smashed into ice-dust. It was all over in only a few minutes.

The children sank to the ground, exhausted. Again they heard the strange whistling noise and saw a million specks of fire rush upwards into the sky. They looked in all directions, but could not discover the cause of this odd happening.

With the silver mountains so close, they set off at first light the next day. Jeremy and Charlotte walked through the snow all morning. There was not a sound to be heard and not a living thing to be seen. Everywhere were the snow-people's houses, all of them lonely and deserted.

In the afternoon the path they were taking started to rise higher and higher through the steep, rocky hills. The freezing air grew even colder as they neared the top. Finally the last part of the climb lay in front of them. It looked so frightening that the children came to a sudden stop. The path led almost straight up, with a wall of rock one side, and a drop, hundreds of metres down on the other. At the most dangerous point, where the path seemed steepest, and was covered with loose stones, it narrowed to only a few centimetres wide.

"There's only room for one of us at a time," said Charlotte, "so I will go first, to test it."

Charlotte started forward. At the narrowest part she had to stop for a moment and close her eyes to shut out the terrifying drop just a few centimetres away from her toes. The snow-filled valley below was such a long way down, that the little houses of the snow-people looked like match-boxes, and the great rocks they had climbed seemed like small pebbles. Then, gritting her teeth, she continued onwards until she found herself on the edge of a wide level plain, at the very top of the mountain.

"Now you," she called. "Come on, Jeremy, it's not as bad as it looks."

Jeremy began to edge his way across, with Twitch treading close behind. All went well at first. Jeremy fixed his eyes on the far side, where Charlotte was waiting, and never once did he look downwards. It was not long before his feet were on the narrowest part.

But, just when it seemed that a few more steps would see him safely across, his foot sent a loose stone bouncing from the path. It clattered and banged against the rocky walls as it went falling, falling down into the depths below. Jeremy couldn't stop himself from looking downwards. Suddenly the narrow path seemed to shift and shake under his feet.

"Look up, Jeremy! Look at me!" Charlotte shouted, but it was no use. Trembling with panic, Jeremy's knees gave way, and he swayed one way and then the other. He lost his balance and toppled over the edge of the cliff, his hands desperately grasping and scrabbling, trying to get a grip of something to save him.

Twitch gave a tremendous leaping bound forward. Lying flat on the narrow ledge, his tail, bushy with fright, flopped over to where Jeremy's fingers were slipping away. Jeremy felt the furry touch upon his hand. His fingers closed round Twitch's tail, and his fall came to a sudden stop.

Twitch dug his claws deeply into the hard ground to stop himself from sliding. "Charlotte," he squalled. "Quickly, I can't hold on for long."

Charlotte dashed back onto the ledge and lay flat on the ground, reaching out to where Twitch was grimly hanging on to Jeremy. She took off the haversack and threw the straps forward. It was no good, they were not quite long enough. Charlotte wriggled a few more centimetres forward, the ledge was so narrow now that, with her side pressed against the cliff wall, she could still feel that her other side was at the very edge of the drop. Once more she threw the straps. This time they fell right in front of Twitch, just near enough for him to push them over the edge so that Jeremy could grasp them.

Now Twitch was free to help Charlotte, so he seized one corner of the haversack. They pulled and heaved and tugged, while Jeremy pushed upwards against the cliff wall with his toes. Gradually, bit by bit they managed to drag him back up

A moment later they were all safely on the wide plain. They realised that they were on the very top of the Silver Mountains. Some distance away, in the centre of the plain, stood the great tower, with the light on the top burning clear.

They were on a vast, level stretch of black rock, smooth and glistening in the starlight, with not a trace of snow. The flame from the tower reflected from the shining rock as if to make a pathway. As they drew nearer, they began to make out a great number of silent, still shapes gathered around the foot of the tower.

"It's the snow-people!" Jeremy exclaimed.

"They are all watching and waiting," Charlotte whispered.

"If only they would make some noise," Jeremy thought to himself, but not a sound, not even a whisper reached them, across the cold, still air, while they walked towards the tower.

The tower was very wide and tall. Jeremy and Charlotte walked all the way round, but they found no opening of any kind. It seemed that the only way to reach the Fire of Achievement was by a narrow, stone staircase that wound upwards, round and round the tower, going on and on until it almost disappeared in the hazy light at the top. The old stone steps were worn and slippery.

As it had looked from the ground, the climb went on and on, round and round, and still with not a sound from the watching snow-people.

After what felt like hours, they took the final step and were, at last, on the absolute top. Jeremy and Charlotte looked in awe at the fire rushing noiselessly upwards from a golden bowl. Something made them draw closer to the flames until, only a foot away they could see, floating in the centre of the bowl, in the heart of the fire, a shining key fashioned of red, flaming jewels.

At first neither dared make a move to reach for it through the burning fire.

Charlotte's head drooped forwards and she covered her face with her hands. "We can never reach the key through those surging, burning flames," she cried softly.

But Jeremy was determined to get it. With no further hesitation, he closed his eyes, plunged his hand deep into the river of fire and grasped the key.

To his amazement, he found there was no heat, no pain, no burning. When he opened his eyes again, the great fire was gone. As he handed the red key to Charlotte it shone with a strange light. Charlotte looked at it for a long time before placing it carefully in the haversack.

At the very moment that she finished wrapping the key with the other, the tower began to move beneath the children's feet. It started to sway and to shake, and then, to their startled surprise, it dissolved around them into great billows of grey dust, which swirled and twisted until blown away by the breeze. Although they had felt themselves to have been so high, at the tower's top, they now found themselves back on the ground with only a tiny bump.

They fell on soft green grass. The sky over their heads was blue, and lit by a warm, golden sun.

"Where's all the snow and ice gone?" asked a puzzled Jeremy.

"What's happened to the black rocks?"

They had little time to wonder. They were suddenly surrounded by the snow-people, all dancing and singing.

"It's almost exactly what happened on Home World," Jeremy said quietly. Charlotte nodded.

"Jeremy and Charlotte," a voice said. "You were sent here to help us, and by your strength and determination you have broken the spells which have made this world such a miserable place to live on."

The children looked in all directions, but they could not see where the voice was coming from. It certainly was not any of the snow-people, for they had such funny little squeaky voices. Looking upwards they saw a faint, misty outline against the blue sky. As they gazed in wonder, the beautiful voice spoke once more.

"All the creatures you've destroyed were made by the Evil Wizard, from the spells that escaped. As the creatures were destroyed they changed back into the original spells and rushed back to him. He is so glad to get them back that he has promised never to do anything so dreadful again."

The voice stopped. The snow-people vanished. In their place were crowds of boys and girls.

"Thank you!" they said. They had also been changed by the escaped spells, turning them into the snow-people. But now everything was back as it had been a long time ago.

What a party there was later that day! Several small waterfalls splashed down the rocks and each one had a different sparkling flavour. The trees were full of wonderful, sweet fruits. For a time Jeremy and Charlotte talked and laughed and played, but they were not allowed to enjoy it all for long. Just when the party seemed to be at its best, a silver bird floated down from the empty blue sky, and gently landed on Jeremy's hand.

"Children," the bird spoke quietly, "you must be on your way."

Without question Charlotte and Jeremy rose to their feet, and followed the tiny bird as it led them towards the side of the mountain. As they approached the shining rocks, the air grew hazy, and the happy laughter faded. As they turned, for a last look, there was nothing to be seen except swirling white clouds.

The bird stopped, the mist cleared and once more the sun shone, but there was no trace of the boys and girls. The mountain too had gone. Everything around seemed different. In front of the children was a tall tree covered with masses of blue and white flowers, and beneath it, the grass was soft and deep.

"Rest now," the voice sang. As it did so, its voice grew fainter. "Rest now, for you will need to be strong tomorrow." Its voice faded away. When the children looked up, the little bird had gone.

WORLD OF AIR

Several hours must have passed when Jeremy, Charlotte and Twitch suddenly awoke. A silvery voice seemed to be speaking from nowhere.

"It's time to go," they heard. "You needed to rest before your next search started, and now you are ready."

The children stood up. The voice continued, "Close your eyes and count to ten."

Charlotte began to count and quickly Jeremy joined in. Twitch hastily jumped into his arms. As the children counted, they felt a strange sensation, a twisting and moving throughout their arms and legs. As they said "Ten!" they suddenly felt a strong breeze blowing, then a soft bump. When they opened their eyes they cried out in wonder. Everything around them had completely changed.

They were standing in a world of billowing and shining clouds which drifted below, above and all around them. Between the clouds in every direction, patches of blue sky shone through. They felt that they were treading on layers of cotton wool, into which their feet sank several inches with every step. Here and there, as they looked down, they were able to see far across space to where a world which they knew was called Earth shimmered.

Jeremy and Charlotte walked along the path that stretched in front of them, the surface feeling soft and spongy beneath their feet. Light was reflecting from the fluffy clouds, and smoky wisps were floating through the air, getting into their hair and mouths and reminding them strongly of bath time, and home.

Twitch was grumbling and groaning. He was not at all happy – every time he bounded forward he sank up to his middle. In the deeper patches, only the tips of his tail, ears and whiskers showed

44

that he was still there.

Bright golden splashes of sunshine glowed through the thinner patches of cloud. Here and there cloud castles floated and gleamed like icing on huge cakes.

Suddenly, round one bend, the path stopped. There was a door at the foot of a very high, fluffy wall, but it was firmly closed, and a notice on it said:

KEEP OUT

"Look," Jeremy said as he peeped through the gaps around the door. "There is a golden castle far away over there."

Then all three of them could hear bells. The chimes came from the castle and seemed to call their names:

"Jeremy! Charlotte! Jeremy! Charlotte!"

"Somehow we must get there," Charlotte said.

They walked around the wall of cloud, but there was no way in. Then they noticed a path leading off between huge, tumbled cloud-banks, and just around the corner there was a sign:

BEWARE! DEVIL LIGHTS AND STORM SPRITES!

"What shall we do?" Jeremy asked Charlotte nervously.

"We must carry on," she answered.

Twitch gave a shaky "Meow" and jumped up to snuggle between the haversack and Charlotte's coat.

And then, suddenly, the path came to an end. Charlotte and Jeremy found themselves at the very edge of the World of Air. In front of them there was only blue sky. Looking down, just a few inches away from their feet, there was nothing!

"Wow!" Jeremy gasped, quickly taking a step back from the edge.

Across the wide blue sky the children could see, here and there, other cloud islands. Some were very near but others were so far away that they were only misty shapes. Mostly they gleamed in silver, or blue, or white and some were even golden tinted. But there were a few that were black and looked angry.

Suddenly, Charlotte shouted: "Look out! One of the black clouds is coming towards us!"

There was a "bump" as it collided with the cloud edge a few feet from where the children stood. Jeremy was thrown off balance and, before either Charlotte or Twitch realised what had happened, he tumbled head over heels, down into the darkness of the black island.

"Help!" Jeremy cried, as strange hands, with long, thin, blue fingers gripped him. He kicked and struggled and screamed, but the fingers wouldn't let go.

"Storm sprites!" he shouted.

The sprites had masses of grey hair, like cotton wool, and tiny mean-looking ice blue eyes. Their noses were thin and curled, with a red bump on the end. In their wide, open mouths Jeremy could see jagged, yellow teeth.

"Get up!" a voice growled.

Jeremy jumped instantly to his feet.

Then the voice rumbled again:

"You're exactly what we've been searching for. You are big and strong, fit to be our slave. We need someone to do all our hard work, to sweep up the heaps of lightning after our storms, and to fetch the pails of stardust for our spells."

This did not sound too bad to Jeremy. "Heaps of lightning?! Pails of stardust!" Jeremy exclaimed excitedly. But he was also thinking of how to escape from these air creatures.

But then everything went black as he was thrown into a huge bag. It was dark and had the same smell as when there has been thunder and lightening in the sky.

"This must be where they store the spare lightning," he said to himself, and at that moment he felt another jerk and realised that the island was now floating rapidly away from the cloud where Charlotte and Twitch stood.

"Jeremy! Jeremy!" he could hear Charlotte shouting until her voice faded away into the distance."

Charlotte sank to the ground and cried. Twitch sat beside her and then, through her tears Charlotte saw a brilliant sparkle of orange light, then red and yellow, and blue, and she found herself surrounded by a host of the most beautiful little creatures she had ever seen.

In every direction were hundreds of tiny, winged horses of every colour. They floated and twirled around like a thousand rainbows. Then, in voices like pattering raindrops mixed with the tinkle of bells, they spoke.

"Please don't cry. The Storm-Sprites are always raiding the cloud islands. They steal us away to make us their slaves. We are made from star-crystals and are so fragile that we cannot fight back, and even a loud noise will shatter us into a million pieces."

"I will try to stop all that," Charlotte promised, "but first of all I must get my brother back!"

"I wouldn't worry if I were you," the first little horse said. Your brother is big and strong. He'll escape."

"But how?" Charlotte asked.

"Surely we'll think of something between us."

"We *shall* beat the sprites," Charlotte said "There must be a way."

She started to think hard. "I do have some enchanted things to help me, in the haversack," she said. "I must be able to use them."

She opened the haversack and took out the Water of Protection and the Magic Mirror, laying them down carefully on the neatly folded Cloak of Invisibility. All the time the horses fluttered around, making small bell-like noises of excitement.

"I know!" Charlotte suddenly exclaimed, clapping her hands.

On doing so she frightened the crystal horses.

"Oh, I am sorry," she said to the horses. "I forgot that noises frighten you. But I think I can find a way to help us all."

The crystal horses flew back to her, and their leader smiled.

"Please, tell us about your plan," they said.

"I have to act as quickly as possible," Charlotte said. "I can't lose any time, even to explain my idea. There'll be a terrible noise, and the sprites will come, so please go away as far as possible. Fly to that rose-coloured island, way over there in the distance, and trust me to do my best."

Twitch had been curled up at Charlotte's feet with his nose tucked into his tail, away from those annoying wisps of cloud that kept tickling him, but hearing Charlotte's words, he realised they were soon going to be on the move. Stretching first one leg, then the other he rose to his feet. The little horses looked at him with some concern – he was easily as big as they were, perhaps even bigger. He must have seemed to them like a black, furry monster. Seeing the way they looked at him he stood up as high as he could, on his back legs, and strutted up and down.

"I'll see that everything goes alright," he said, looking his fiercest and bravest.

Unknown to Twitch, one of the younger ones had crept up behind him.

"BOO! BOO!" it shouted suddenly, in its high, tinkling voice. In one bound Twitch was hiding inside Charlotte's coat. All the horses laughed, and Charlotte found it difficult not to do so herself.

Peeping out from the coat cautiously, Twitch said, "I was just testing to see if Charlotte was alright."

Charlotte pretended to believe, giving Twitch a big hug, and saying "Thank you."

So, still laughing, the horses flew away like a cloud of fairy lights.

Charlotte made her way back down the dark path, past the

"Danger" notice to where, far away in the distance she could just make out a tiny black dot – the island of black clouds.

"The best thing for me to do," she said to Twitch, "is to let the Storm-Sprites see me so that they will want to capture me too."

She then began to jump up and down, with her arms up in the air so that the sprites could see her.

"It's working!" Charlotte shouted. The black cloud was coming nearer and nearer. Soon it was close enough for Charlotte to see the sprites' angry faces. Quickly she gathered Twitch in her arms and put on the Cloak of Invisibility. In one small jump she landed lightly on the cloud of the storm sprites.

The raiding party of the sprites were rushing about everywhere. Not two minutes ago they had seen their intended victim but now they couldn't find her. Charlotte could hear them shrieking and shouting at each other angrily. They even started to fight among themselves.

The black island floated swiftly away from the beautiful glowing world of Air. Charlotte could hear loud rumbling noises through the gloomy clouds that now pressed in tightly all around. The sprites were moving down a dark, tunnel-like pathway between jet-black boiling clouds. At the end of the path, Charlotte saw a deep, dark hole. One by one the sprites disappeared over the edge and floated gently downwards.

With no further thought she stepped forward, feeling Twitch groan with dismay. She found herself slowly drifting down, like a feather floating on still air. In a very short time her feet quietly touched the bottom. Still hidden within the Cloak of Invisibility she looked around.

It was difficult to see much from where she stood, for her view was blocked by great, tumbled, cloud-boulders. It took her and Twitch several minutes to find their way through. Suddenly spread out in full view was a scene from the wildest of all nightmares. Everywhere were huge, black pots, and in each one, fierce fires were burning, some with red flames, some green, and some blue. But the strangest thing was that there was no heat – the fires were completely cold.

The pot with the blue fire attracted Charlotte's attention the most.

It was far larger than any of the others, and the blue fire shimmered and twisted into strange shapes. At times it bubbled over the edge and snapped into a thousand silvery sparks. Odd shapes hovered and flitted in the air all around. A low humming noise filled Charlotte's ears, making them buzz and ache slightly, as if she were under water. Now and then silver fire shot into the air from the pots, flashing here, there, everywhere, until it slowly faded away.

Gradually Charlotte became aware of a dull, booming sound. Turning her head she saw, over on the far side, a colossal pot made of a grey, misty material, with clouds of thick smoke rising into the air every time the pot boomed. In the air, on the pots and all over the ground were thousands of storm sprites. They scurried to and fro, here and there, endlessly gathering together all sorts of peculiar coloured objects. All the time they were spitting and scratching hatefully at one another.

"Where can Jeremy be?" Charlotte whispered to Twitch. Together they examined every corner of the great wide pit in which they stood. Their search was not made any easier by the clouds of smoke drifting in all directions.

"But surely he MUST be here," she said to Twitch. "This is where all the work is being done!"

As she searched the gloomy shadows she noticed a very high cloud-boulder with sides that could easily be climbed. "We might be able to see better from the top of that," she said.

It took only half a minute to climb the soft, clammy side. With Twitch in her arms, she stood high on the very top. From this new position Charlotte again searched every corner of the great work-place.

"There he is!" She said in a loud whisper that made Twitch jump.

Jeremy was in a dark corner, fastened by a long, thin chain. He was carrying strange, heavy looking objects. He stopped every now and again to stir the bubbling pots.

"Come on, Twitch, time for action," she said.

They clambered down from the boulder and edged their way across the crowded workshop towards Jeremy. All the time they had to dodge the rushing, scurrying crowds of sprites.

"Watch out!" Twitch whispered, as Charlotte nearly got splashed with green fire when she came too close to the pots.

They were very near Jeremy when two sprites close by started to fight. One gave the other a great blow which quite knocked it off its feet. The sprite rolled backwards across the floor and the next moment collided heavily with Charlotte. The creature jumped to its feet, snarling and screeching with anger, and turned to attack. But, of course, there was no one to be seen. There was no one to be felt for either. Charlotte had quickly jumped out of the way after the collision. The look of surprise on the sprites' faces almost made Charlotte laugh out loud.

The sprites searched first one way, then the other. They stretched their long fingers out to touch the air, high, low, both sides. But Charlotte kept well out of the way. At last they gave up, and went off angrily to get on with their work.

Charlotte saw the look of surprise in Jeremy's face. He stopped working and looked around.

Suddenly a great shout came. "Get on with your work, slave, or you will be thrown into the blue fire of the electric sparks."

Jeremy bent down to lift the jagged bar of silver metal that lay at his feet. Charlotte had managed, at last, to get really close to him. She could see how tired Jeremy was, covered in grey dust, and with cuts and bruises on his arms and legs.

Leaning over, close to Jeremy's ear, she whispered, "Jeremy, it's me, Charlotte. You won't be working here much longer, I promise you."

Jeremy nearly jumped out of his skin.

"Don't be afraid, "Charlotte continued. "Stand still."

Jeremy stood absolutely still whilst Charlotte took the Water of Protection from the haversack. Very carefully, she poured a tiny drop onto the chain that held Jeremy captive. In a silent sparkle the chain dissolved into nothing.

"Quickly! Come under the cloak," Charlotte whispered urgently, and in two seconds Jeremy had disappeared. The first part of Charlotte's plan had worked.

The children now cautiously started to make their way through the hoards of sprites towards the far side of the workshop, where they could see a path leading upwards. They were most of the way across when the sprites saw the broken chain and realised that Jeremy had escaped. They started screeching and shouting, making a terrible noise. From every corner of the great pit poured hundreds of furious, screaming sprites, seething and boiling with rage, and all blaming each other for Jeremy's escape.

At long last the children found themselves safely on the path. They were a little way along it when Jeremy suddenly stopped.

"Where's Twitch?" he cried, looking around anxiously.

"Isn't he behind you?" asked Charlotte. "I thought he was following when we left the other side of this place."

Too late, Charlotte and Jeremy noticed that there was a big commotion in the far corner.

"The sprites have found him!" Charlotte said.

Twitch had been seized in the sprites' claw-like fingers, and was being taken to the great pot of blue fire.

"They're going to drop him in," wailed Jeremy in terror. "We've got to do something."

Charlotte had already decided what to do: she dashed out from under the magic cloak, and shouted, "Fight, Twitch, fight!"

In surprise at Charlotte's sudden appearance from nowhere, the sprites loosened their hold on Twitch. At once he turned into a raging ball of black, tearing, scratching fury. For a moment the sprites let go, and Twitch fell downwards, twisting himself over in mid-air. He ran as fast as he could all the way across the workshop.

But the sprites were fast too and got to Charlotte before she had time to go under the Cloak of Invisibility again. They tore at her hair, scratched at her eyes and threw streams of sparks from the tips of their fingers. Charlotte sank to the ground, dropping the haversack as she did so.

Jeremy knew there was only one thing to do. He tore open the haversack and took out the mirror. As he held it out towards the sprites, a small red light started to glow deep within.

The red glow grew brighter, and still brighter and a sword of light flashed towards the pot of green fire. The bubbling liquid in the pot boiled more furiously and started to spill over, onto the silver flames beneath. A purple steam rose into the air as the pot began to hiss and rumble. Suddenly, cracks appeared in its sides, and all around, the other pots too began to boil over. There were clouds of steam, and out of them came shapes of all colours. It all made a terrible noise.

The storm sprites screamed and shrieked as they saw all these terrible spells getting out of control. In a mad rush they tried to fight their way out of the pit to safety, but the magic steam in the air imprisoned them, and they could no longer fly.

Not waiting to see any more, Jeremy, Charlotte and Twitch raced up the path as the noise from behind grew even louder.

They had just managed to reach the top when there was a terrible explosion below, as all the pots blew up. The clouds of smoke around them were lit up by huge flashes of lightning.

Some sprites had managed to get to the top too. Their faces were ugly and they looked furious.

"Faster! Faster!" Charlotte called out to Jeremy.

At last they got to the end of the path. But then they were still trapped. The gleaming sides of the white clouds of the World of Air were hundreds of feet away. It was much too far for them to jump across.

"Charlotte looked behind her and shouted, "Look out! The sprites are getting nearer."

"We'll fight them off, said Jeremy bravely.

Jeremy and Charlotte prepared themselves to face the sprites. But, almost as the first eager hands clutched at Jeremy, from the white clouds came hundreds of the crystal horses. The children saw that they were carrying, on silver threads, a small, round golden platform, so light and delicate that it swayed this way and that with every gentle breeze.

"Jump," the tinkling voices called. "Jeremy, Charlotte, jump quickly."

The children wasted no time. They jumped forward and landed lightly on the golden platform.

In an instance the crystal horses drew it up high into the cloudy sky. Jeremy and Charlotte were out of the reach of the sprites, at last.

Another explosion, this time far away, drew the children's attention back to the black world they had just left. Something strange was happening. Deep within the dark, boiling clouds, gleamed flickers of fire – red, green and blue – growing brighter and brighter, and leaping up fiercely against the blackness behind.

The sprites were now standing in absolute silence, their backs turned to the children as they studied the strange fires with obvious unease. The weird flames became brighter, and leaped higher into the sky.

The horses knew that something terrible was about to happen. They stopped pulling the platform and turned to watch. The whole sky was alight with the glare from the black cloud.

Everything seemed to happen at once. An enormous clap of thunder ripped and exploded through the cloud banks of the world of the storm sprites. The green, blue and red flames flickered and crackled in a hundred rivers of fire throughout the black island and the children found their eyes dazzled by the brilliant light. A roaring, tearing rumble went on and on.

A flash of lightning ripped across the sky. A hurricane of wind took control of the golden platform, tearing it free from the horses and sending it dipping and swaying at a tremendous speed. It was nearly impossible for the children to avoid being thrown off. When they felt they could hold on no longer, the platform came to a violent stop. Jeremy and Charlotte were flung off, head over heels into the middle of a big, fleecy, white cloud.

The children slowly rose to their feet.

"Look!" Jeremy exclaimed. "We're back in the white clouds of the World of Air."

Then they both looked across the sky to where the black island should be. The evil black island no longer existed. Instead there were thousands of small clouds which were being blown in different directions. The sprites were scattered across the hundreds of small clouds.

"I don't think they'll be able to cause any more trouble now," Charlotte said.

"They will only be able to make some small storms, anyway,"

Jeremy added.

The crystal horses clustered around the children, singing and laughing. Their beautiful colours flashed even more brilliantly than ever before. At last, they could live in peace, and play, and float in the sunshine without thought of destruction or capture.

There was a great party that evening. The crystal horses gathered to sing and dance, and to thank the children for what they had done.

Twitch proudly stalked round and round, telling tales of how he had punched and scratched the sprites.

As Jeremy and Charlotte sat there, happily watching and listening, they heard their names called by a small group of horses the far side of the cloud-meadow. Then more of the horses joined in, calling their names.

"Jeremy and Charlotte. Jeremy and Charlotte. Come over here."

The children stood up and looked across to where hundreds of the crystal horses were gathered. Over and around the gathering glowed a pale, rose-coloured light which grew steadily brighter.

As if from nowhere a voice spoke, and all the horses became absolutely silent and still.

"I am the Queen of the World of Air," the voice said. For a long time I have grieved over the attacks by the terrible storm sprites, but I have been powerless to prevent them. I shall always be grateful to you for your bravery in fighting and defeating the sprites. None of us here will ever forget you."

Neither Jeremy nor Charlotte knew what to say, because they had never spoken to a Queen before. For a moment there was silence until, once again the children heard the Queen's silvery voice.

"Look carefully," the voice said quietly. "Look at the moonbeam table, and do not be afraid."

The children gasped in amazement. In an open space, surrounded by the watching horses and at the foot of a shaft of moonlight, a small, shining table gradually appeared. The little horses drew back and formed a great multi-coloured ring of brilliance around the table.

Slowly the children walked forwards A brilliant shaft of

moonlight seemed to turn the table into a bowl of silver fire. Then the moonbeam was gone. Now the table itself was gleaming and glowing with a thousand threads of light, all of which were flowing from a star-like object on the centre of the table – and Charlotte and Jeremy saw with excitement that the star-like object was a beautifully fashioned, glittering silver key.

GOLDEN CASTLE

The crystal horses began to leave. Each one came to thank Jeremy and Charlotte.

"Thank you," a beautiful white horse said, "and best of luck in finding the Golden Castle."

"Golden Castle!" Jeremy exclaimed, turning to Charlotte, but she looked just as puzzled.

"Yes, that's your next stop," the horse replied.

When the last horse had gone, Jeremy, Charlotte and Twitch sat quietly in the moonlight, thinking of the silver key now safely hidden away with the others. They talked about how they would get to the Golden Castle.

"Think about that tomorrow," Twitch said as he curled up round Jeremy. "It's bed time now."

So the three snuggled down on the soft white cloud and went to sleep.

They woke up early the next morning and started making plans.

"There's a great wall around the castle," Charlotte said. "Perhaps Twitch could climb up and throw us a rope."

"No," said Jeremy. "I've got an idea. Do you remember how the crystal horses brought us from the black cloud?"

"On that floating golden platform, you mean?"

"Yes. Maybe they could do the same again, only this time we'd go over the castle wall."

"That's not a bad idea," Charlotte said.

"Let's go and look for the crystal horses, then." Jeremy said.

But when Jeremy and Charlotte explained about their plan to the horses, they looked very serious. They began to talk in whispers to one another. Finally, the white crystal horse said, "We can help you as you wish, but you must be very careful. The mighty comet blazer lives there. When he's in a bad mood, no one dares to go near him."

"We'll be careful," replied Charlotte. "But as you realise, whatever the danger, we have to go."

"As soon as we can," Jeremy added.

The horses nodded.

"Can we go, then?" Jeremy asked.

"Yes," the white horse replied. "We'll go and collect the floating platform."

While the children waited, Charlotte opened the haversack and checked through the contents, making quite sure that the keys were secure and all the magic items were easy to get at.

Soon they could see the horses coming back with the golden cloud-platform. It floated just a few feet from the ground. Carefully the children stepped up onto the shining platform. It shifted slowly in the faint breeze. Twitch, who hated heights, clung tightly to Charlotte, with his eyes firmly closed.

The horses released the floating platform, and it rose higher and higher. Hundreds of crystal horses flashed and sparkled around in every direction.

The cloud platform came near the castle wall. It went up and up, but the wall was so high that it seemed as if it would never end. On and on, higher and higher, still the golden platform continued to rise, until the children thought that it would go on forever.

But, all of a sudden the wall ended. Looking down, Jeremy and Charlotte could at last see over the top. But everything was white, flat and featureless, like a huge sheet of icing on a cake.

"Now we must go," chimed those horses who had remained with the children. "We dare not come any further. Good-bye, we shall never forget you"

"Good-bye," said Jeremy and Charlotte.

The platform began to go down very quickly, and in only a minute or two it landed with a small bump on the flat, white surface. As the children rolled over, and jumped to their feet the platform rose rapidly into the air, and was gone.

The three travellers turned towards the wondrous castle shimmering and blazing in the sun. It seemed further away than they had imagined. It also looked much bigger now that they were on the same side of the wall.

"Come on," said Jeremy

The three set off steadily, across the strange, white plain. The sun shone strong on their heads. The glistening on the ground made their eyes ache.

After they had been travelling for about an hour Charlotte felt an odd sensation. She turned to Jeremy and said, "I can't see very clearly."

"Nor me," replied Jeremy.

Twitch was sitting unhappily, with his tail curled tightly around his body, and his paws over his eyes.

In front of them, the air seemed to thicken. The ground shivered beneath their feet. Suddenly, with a frightening jolt, the flat ground on which they stood fell downwards into a steep slope. The three of them tumbled around and about, this way and that, head over heels. They finally stopped. The air above them darkened into blackness.

"The castle!" Charlotte exclaimed.

"It's disappeared," Jeremy said.

Around them everything had changed – the sky, the ground and the smells.

"We're not in the World of Air anymore," Jeremy said sadly.

Around them were tree trunks. They were in the middle of what looked like a dark forest.

"Where's the haversack?" Charlotte asked as they both stood up and started to look for it.

Twitch found it; it had been caught in a giant thorn. Anxiously, Charlotte looked inside. "It's all here!" she said.

"Thank goodness!" Jeremy said. "Check it."

"Yes, all here, look: the keys, the Cloak of Invisibility, the Water of Protection and the Magic Mirror."

Then they looked at the forest around them again. A brighter patch seemed to glimmer faintly at the far end of a long tunnel of trees.

"It must be that way," Jeremy said.

Without further words they all set off along the wet, cold and muddy pathway. The rustling and whispering trees crowded closely around, making them look over their shoulders all the time.

It was a long and uncomfortable walk. With great relief the children at last stepped out of the forest onto a narrow roadway. It was paved with huge, rough flagstones, and edged with high, thorny hedges. The thorny branches seemed to reach out in an attempt to seize the three travellers. Keeping well in the middle, the children followed the winding road, across a flat land of dreary fields. The road was wet, almost covered by huge puddles. Some of them looked as if they had no bottom.

The children trudged on and on. All the time it drizzled, and their clothes were getting soaking wet. But they were taken completely by surprise when they turned a sharp bend. In front of them was the biggest puddle of all. It was so wide it looked almost like a lake. The road was blocked completely, from one side to another.

They searched the water's edge carefully, but it reached right up to the foot of the thorn-filled hedge, with its twisting, reaching branches. There was no way to jump over –

"There must be a way to cross it," Jeremy said to himself.

"Yes," said Charlotte as she looked round. "I've just found out how."

"How?" asked Jeremy.

"See that fallen tree, over there?" She pointed to an old, rotten tree by the roadside. "If we can get it into the water it might reach to the other side."

For a long time they fought and struggled with the heavy old tree, getting scratched and covered with mud. Strange beetles and spiders ran out from the centre of the trunk, making Jeremy and Charlotte jump.

At last, the tree was in the water. It stretched safely from where the roadway ended, across the water, and to the other side.

They started to cross straight away. It was a frightening experience. The tree was slippery, and its decayed surface was loose and breaking away. It rocked and shook under the weight of the children. But there was worse to come.

Half way across, the water began to ripple and swirl. In an instance it seemed to boil with the thrashing movements of thousands of red and blue fish.

"Bone-suckers!" Charlotte shouted. "The crystal horses warned us about them."

"Are they the ones that stick to your legs and eat through your bones?" Jeremy asked. But Charlotte didn't have time to answer. Hundreds of fish filled the lake. They thrust their tooth-filled snouts out of the water in desperate efforts to reach the children.

The children were surrounded by the red and blue brilliant flashing of the fish's bodies.

"Oh no!" Charlotte cried out. In all directions, there were many more ponds, full of the terrible fish, all of them jumping and leaping wildly out of the water.

It all became too much for Twitch. In panic he twisted free from the safety of Charlotte's arms and leaped wildly for dry land. For a moment the children thought he had landed safely, but then, with a wail of despair, he fell back and disappeared into the middle of the great hoards of greedy fish.

Without a moment's hesitation, Jeremy plunged into the water. With one great scoop, he took hold of Twitch and threw the cat high into the air. Twitch landed on the other side of the puddle.

Hundreds of fish gathered round Jeremy, but he kept them away by kicking and splashing. In frantic haste Charlotte reached into the haversack for the Magic Mirror.

"Here it goes," she shouted. But her fingers were shaking so much that she could not hold it, and with a small splash it dropped and slid silently into the dark water.

Charlotte started to cry, but almost instantly she saw that the water around the Mirror began to bubble and boil. Huge clouds of steam rose into the air, covering the entire surface of the water.

The Bone-suckers were in a state of panic. Charlotte, taking advantage of this, jumped into the water and, grasped Jeremy's arm. She pushed and pulled him up the bank and onto dry land. Several of the blue and red fish already had their teeth into his arms and legs. Charlotte took one of her shoes and hit the fish, knocking them off.

Then, as Charlotte was putting her shoe back on, she cried out in fright. The entire lake burst into a fantastic rushing, roaring, spout of steam and exploded high up into the air. It sounded like a thousand kettles of water boiling at the same time. The water then fell back to the ground in every direction.

But then something magic happened: all the drops carried a fragment of the Mirror. So, wherever they fell, the magic fell too, causing the waters everywhere to boil and explode in giant thunderstorms.

The air was filled with steam. Neither Charlotte nor Jeremy could see a thing.

"That should destroy the bone-suckers," Charlotte said.

At last the noises stopped. A great silence fell over the whole countryside and a gentle breeze blew the clouds of steam away, cooling and refreshing the air. All the muddy ponds and puddles were gone. The ground was dry and firm.

Jeremy and Charlotte were so filled with relief that they started chasing Twitch around and playing all sorts of games. At first they didn't notice the many small and strange creatures who had gathered to watch them.

It was Twitch who saw them first, and he fell backwards from the tree-trunk in astonishment. "Look, Charlotte, look," he spluttered.

Both children turned round.

"Hello," Charlotte said, delighted to see so many animals.

That did it. All the animals started to speak together, in squeaks and chirrups, growls and grunts. The children laughed, because it sounded so funny. But as quickly as it had started, it stopped.

"Look!" It was Jeremy's time to be surprised. Out of nowhere a strange little man appeared. He was about as tall as Charlotte's knee, and was wearing a red hat, green trousers and black water boots.

"It's a Wood Gnome," Charlotte whispered to Jeremy. "I know it is. I've seen a picture of one in an old book, long ago, in the Woodcutter's hut."

The gnome frowned. "Stop whispering," he said sharply. "It's rude!"

Charlotte nodded. "I'm sorry," she replied. "I won't do it again."

The wood gnome smiled and said, "That's quite alright. I didn't mean to snap at you. In fact I wanted to thank you for what you've done. I watched you crossing the lake. I'm so glad that all the water-homes of the bone-sucker fish were destroyed. All of us here want to give you this," and he handed Charlotte a small object. "It's a charm, to help you on your way."

Charlotte looked at the object more carefully. It was a tiny, wooden carving and looked exactly like the gnome himself. As she turned it, she saw that on the back was a faintly glowing white star.

"I've filled this carving with enchantment," said the Gnome. "Every creature here has given a little of his magic to help. If you are ever in real trouble, touch the star and wish hard."

"Thank you very much," said Charlotte and Jeremy together.

"I must be going," the gnome said, and without another word he disappeared.

Charlotte opened the haversack and tucked the little wooden gnome inside. Then she turned to Jeremy and Twitch and said, "We must look for the Magic Mirror."

The furry animals began to talk again and run here and there, trying to help.

But there was no trace of the Mirror left.

"It's gone," said Jeremy, sadly.

"It's saved us enough times," Charlotte added. "Well, we must carry on. Good bye, and thank you," she said to the animals.

"Good bye," said Jeremy.

They set off again along the dry, dusty path. They grew hot and tired, until they felt they could hardly take another step.

"We don't seem to be getting anywhere," groaned Jeremy.

"Just another corner, you'll see," Charlotte said, trying to cheer him up." Round the next bend."

To her surprise, she was right. As they turned the next bend, there in the distance glittered the Golden Castle. It looked very much closer now.

"I can see the windows of the castle," Charlotte said.

"And the doors," Jeremy added.

Charlotte spoke again, "The castle looks as if it's floating."

"It can't be. Look at those enormous stones that make up the walls," Jeremy said.

The road began to descend into a deep and shaded valley, between high, brown hills. Far away in the valley the children could see movement, though they couldn't make out exactly what it was.

They went on walking until night began to fall.

"Let's stop here under this tree," Charlotte said to Jeremy and Twitch.

The three curled up under the protection of the friendly tree, warm inside their cloaks, and they fell asleep.

It was late when Jeremy, Charlotte and Twitch awoke the following morning. The sun was high in the sky as they set off again across the valley. As they walked down the steep, sloping path, the rocky sides began to tower above their heads, blocking the sun and throwing dark shadows across the way.

There were many loose stones on the road, some shining and gleaming with many colours. Several times Jeremy bent to pick up one or two of the prettier stones, but oddly, as soon as he lifted them from the ground, they changed to a dull, muddy colour. Charlotte thought hard about this, and it did not take her long to work out the reason.

"It must be the way they protect themselves," she told Jeremy, "If they remained bright and attractive, people would keep them. But if they change to an ugly brown, they are thrown straight back onto the road."

"They are not really stones then," said Jeremy thoughtfully. "They must be alive."

"Yes, they must be," said Charlotte.

Hearing this, Twitch, who had been jumping from one coloured stone to another, now started to walk carefully between them.

They walked until late afternoon. They were really tired and hungry, when they turned yet another bend. There they stopped and opened their magic sandwich box. As they did so they noticed a bushy tree thickly covered with red and blue berries.

"Don't eat them!" Charlotte warned the others. "They may be poisonous." So they stood, looking longingly at the juicy fruit in front of them.

Just then there was a loud chirruping and twittering. Out of the dull sky, a crowd of small brown birds flew down, into the tree and in no time were eating the fruit, as fast as they could. They also fed their young ones, stuffing berries down their beaks.

Charlotte watched carefully. Soon she realised that the birds never touched the red berries, but only took the blue ones.

"The birds wouldn't eat the berries if they were dangerous – let alone feed them to their babies," Charlotte said. Cautiously, she picked one of the blue berries and took a tiny bite.

It was unbelievable! The berry tasted exactly like her favourite breakfast, scrambled eggs! She took a handful, filling her mouth, and yes, she had not imagined it. The taste was just like a big spoonful of scrambled egg, cooked exactly as she liked it.

Jeremy and Twitch were watched anxiously. With her mouth full of berries, Charlotte nodded to them. Needing no second invitation, Jeremy and Twitch started filling their mouths with the berries.

"Marvellous!" Jeremy said to himself, for the taste was terrific. "Porridge! With golden syrup." He couldn't eat fast enough.

No matter how many berries they took from the tree, the branches always remained full.

"Meow," Twitch said. "Herrings!"

They ate till they thought they would burst. They were so tired from their long walk, that they lay down to rest. The song of the birds and the warm air made their heads nod and their eyes heavy. Soon they were fast asleep.

An hour passed, then two. The sun climbed higher in the sky until it was completely overhead. Jeremy woke up, feeling very hot. He sat up, rubbing his eyes.

"Gosh!" he said. "We've been asleep for ages." He shook Charlotte's arm. She immediately woke up and jumped to her feet.

"Oh dear," she cried. "We must try to get through the valley before nightfall."

Thanks to their rest, they were able to walk quite fast. The pathway was lit by the bright sun, and it all seemed very pleasant and enjoyable. There was a small hill, and as they came to the top the path opened up into a wide, open field.

The field was full of the weirdest objects they had ever seen. There were enormous rocks everywhere. But there were also huge things that looked like great, black wheels, with pink and red centres. They also had blue spokes that rippled and shivered the whole time. The strange wheels were rolling about and crashing into the rocks, into the trees and into each other.

They moved with great speed, and each time they collided with anything, there was a brilliant spark, a deafening crashing noise and a thick spurt of black oily smoke. The smoke made the children cough and choke

"Why on earth are those things crashing about so madly?" wondered Charlotte out loud.

As she spoke, a small, white rabbit dashed from a hole in the rocks and ran straight in front of one of the wheels. The wheel skidded to a stop, and sparks flashed all around the little creature. In a moment it faded away to nothing. All that was left was a puff of black smoke.

"Eaten by the wheel!" Jeremy shouted in horror. " How are we going to get past them? They're blocking the path. Will they stop moving about?"

"No," Charlotte answered. "Not while they are eating!"

And the wheels were eating everything. Rocks, trees, each other, and any creatures near enough were all being eaten, after they had been broken into small pieces by the terrible sparks. "Let's get away from here, or we'll be eaten too," cried Jeremy.

"There's no other path," said Charlotte.

The burning sun shone down and beat upon the children's heads as they stood there, unable to decide what to do. Every now and again, a small white cloud floated across the blue sky. Over in the distance, a band of bigger, darker clouds was approaching. Soon deep shadow spread across the valley and reached the field.

As the dark shadow covered the wheels, they slowed to a halt and became quiet and still. They remained so until, after only a second or two, the sun came out again. Then, in an instant they were dashing and sparking fiercely once more.

A thicker cloud came. It lasted several minutes. Again the Wheels stopped moving and Charlotte realised that they only moved while the sun was shining.

"I've got an idea," she said. "If we wait for a really huge cloud, we might be able to dodge between the wheels while they are standing still."

Anxiously they examined the sky. There were many clouds floating around, but they all looked quite small. None were big enough to give more than a few seconds of shadow.

"Why can't we use the Cloak of Invisibility?" Jeremy asked.

"It's not big enough for all three of us."

At long last a larger, blacker cloud floated over the hill. It was not as big as Charlotte would have wished, but she decided that there was no use in waiting any longer.

"We'll have to try now," Charlotte said.

As the cloud began to cover the sun, the children made their way down to the edge of the red, dusty field. As soon as the wheels stopped moving, Jeremy shouted: "Now!"

At full speed they began to dash across the field. The huge black wheels were everywhere, and seemed to be silently glaring at the children as they scampered between them. The heat coming from them was terrible, and puffs of smoke made the children feel ill.

"Stop, Jeremy!" Charlotte suddenly screamed.

The pathway in front of them was completely blocked by a giant wheel, the biggest of them all. It towered above them, silent and still, only the blue spoke-like colours moved. They flickered and twined like snakes as if eager to reach out and crush the three travellers.

The children started to creep round the awful monster. Just at the worst possible moment, Jeremy tripped over his shoe-lace, which was always coming undone. He fell with a "thump" against the side of the wheel.

"Ouch!" Jeremy cried. "It's hot!"

The Wheel shuddered and creaked. For a moment Jeremy couldn't move. The spongy wheel went still again. Jeremy quickly jumped to his feet and raced after the others.

It was then that the wind changed direction. To the children's horror the wind started to blow the clouds sideways, and in seconds the sun had returned. Immediately, the wheels started moving again.

Jeremy and Charlotte looked around for somewhere to hide, but there didn't seem to be anywhere at all. Then Twitch's sharp eyes spotted a tiny cave under a low rock, and as quickly as they could, they dashed towards it.

They rushed into the cave and looked back: outside the monstrous wheels crashed and ground around in fury, trying to get into the cave. Fortunately the rocks hung too low. But such was the mad rage of the monster's attacks, that trickles of dust, and small stones constantly tumbled from the rocky roof a few inches above Charlotte and Jeremy's heads. They could not move, but the wheels could not reach them. For a while nothing changed.

Suddenly, the rock over the children's heads shook, shook again and moved slightly.

"The cave is callapsing" shouted Charlotte.

"We shall be caught!" groaned Jeremy.

It was Twitch who came to their rescue again. With a twist and a jump he struggled free from Charlotte's arm, and ran quickly between the great wheels which were rushing and crashing in every direction. He was so fast and nimble that, try as they might, the wheels could not get near him. But as he leaped from rock to rock, one of the smaller, faster creatures almost seized hold of him.

"Twitch. Twitch," screamed Charlotte. "Look out!"

The warning came just in time. Twitch gave a huge cat-jump and landed right on top of the biggest wheel of them all – the one that Jeremy had bumped into.

The monster stopped still for a moment. This was too much! It went mad with anger. First one way, then the other, backwards and forwards it rolled and thundered. No matter what it did it couldn't reach the cat. Hundreds of the other wheels came roaring up, pushing and crashing in their attempts to knock Twitch down.

Jeremy stood, wide-eyed, watching Twitch. He shivered, for he suddenly felt cold. It took a few seconds for him to realise why. "Charlotte, Charlotte, the wind has changed," he cried out. "It's blowing on us again and soon the cloud will be back"

He was right. Another thick, black cloud drifted across the sun, casting its giant shadow over the wheels. Once again they skidded to a stop, so quickly that Twitch lost his balance and fell with an annoyed "Meow" down to the hard ground.

The children dashed from their cave, and with Twitch held firmly in Charlotte's arms, they rushed along the pathway. At last they reached its furthest end and were safely out of the terrible valley.

They were only just in time. The last cloud floated away and the sun shone fiercely again. The wheels' raging fury reached a new madness that brought the children to a halt. They watched as the dreadful creatures crashed and flashed with rage. The thick, black smoke rose high into the air, twisting and twining into strange devil-like shapes. The children took one last, fearful glance behind them as the path rounded a bend and the valley finally disappeared from their view.

A couple of minutes later Jeremy and Charlotte came to a stop again. Only a short distance in front of them was a gate. It wasn't just an ordinary gate, but a gleaming, shining, golden gate leading directly into the great Golden Castle.

The gate was slightly open. Jeremy gave it a gentle push. Noiselessly it swung wide.

Inside they saw a huge, wide hall which appeared to be made of smoky-blue glass, with shining white walls sparkling all over as though full of stars. The roof was so high that it was lost in a blue misty haze, far above their heads. There was no sign at all of anyone living there.

The floor was bare and empty. As they tiptoed across the strange, glassy surface they looked around wide-eyed, in all directions. Their footsteps echoed as they crossed the great empty space. Then Charlotte came to a sudden halt.

"Jeremy," she said in an excited whisper, "I've just remembered. The Comet Blazer. This must be his home. I wonder where he is. I hope he's not horrible to us!"

"He's not here, that's for sure," replied Jeremy, looking around the great empty hall. He marched off towards the far side, where he had noticed a small door. Charlotte and Twitch followed him.

As the children reached it, they saw there were words carved deep into the wood, words that twisted and blurred as they tried to read them.

"Beware!" Charlotte read out loud.

"Beware of what?" asked Jeremy

"I've no idea." Charlotte replied.

Jeremy peeped round the edge of the door and saw a long, dark passage with a bright light shining a long, long way off. It looked quite a distance – perhaps because the passageway was completely dark!

"Shall we go ahead?" Jeremy asked cautiously.

"Well, there's no other door from the great hall," Charlotte answered. "It looks quiet enough."

As they started walking the door behind them slammed shut, with a noise like thunder. The darkness was even thicker than before.

For a while the children marched along in total silence, eyes fixed on the light ahead. After a time they began to notice an odd rustling noise coming from above their heads. They took no notice, at first, but gradually, the noise became louder.

"What's that noise?" Charlotte asked.

"I don't know. I can't see anything," Jeremy replied. Turning to Twitch he asked, "Can you see anything, Twitch?"

"Meow! No," Twitch replied.

"I though cats could see in the dark." But as Jeremy was finishing his sentence, there was a rush of wings.

Charlotte jumped in alarm as she felt something brush against her hair. "Jeremy!" She just had time to call out to Jeremy before she sank slowly to the ground.

71

Jeremy felt her fall to the floor. He rushed to her side and helped her to her feet, urging her onwards towards the distant light. But she did not seem to have any idea where to go. She walked as if she was asleep, staring ahead. No matter how hard Jeremy tried, she ignored all his questions and remained completely silent.

Suddenly, in the air above the rustling noise came again . As it did so, something lightly touched Jeremy's hair. Instantly he whirled the heavy haversack around, up and above his head. With a hard, jolting thump it hit something so heavily that it was almost torn from his hands. There was "bump" and a huge object crashed to the ground. It lay silently beside him.

In the dim light, Jeremy tried to make out what it was. Gradually, as his eyes became more used to the gloom, he began to recognise the shape which still lay, unmoving, just a few feet away. It was huge flying creature, with the body of a lizard and the head of a vulture. But the most horrible thing about it was its sickly, white colour, which reminded him of something partly decayed. A horrible smell filled the air around the creature, making Jeremy feel quite sick. But he had little time to think about his discomfort. He could plainly hear a gathering of the creatures overhead.

"It must have been one of these that attacked Charlotte," Jeremy said to Twitch. "If only we had the Magic Mirror still," he sighed sadly, "or even the Water of Protection."

"You've got the Wood Gnome," Twitch reminded him.

"Yes!" With all haste he opened the haversack. But, although he looked into every corner, it was not there.

"Where can it be?" he cried.

"In Charlotte's pocket?" Twitch replied.

"Of course! It must be." Jeremy searched her pockets.

"It's here!" In a second he lifted it and pressed the magic star on its back.

The air was still full of the sound of wings, all the time getting closer. Jeremy held the wooden carving above his head, hoping and praying that something would happen soon.

For a moment nothing did. Then, from the eyes of the little

wooden gnome, a pale blue flicker of flame appeared. It climbed into the air, touching the floor and walls of the passage. It crawled across the roof, exploding into the air until the whole passageway was filled with glowing, throbbing clouds of blue fire.

Jeremy clutched Charlotte's hand and sank to the floor, pulling her down too. The blue fire surrounded the flying creatures who desperately tried to escape, flapping in every direction, colliding with one another, crashing into the roof and the sides of the passageway.

One by one the flames surrounded the evil creatures, swirling and wrapping around them, and one by one they exploded in great clouds of green smoke. Soon the air was empty. All of the creatures had been destroyed.

All that remained, besides the smoking heaps of skin and fur was the huge creature that Jeremy had knocked to the ground. It had escaped the blue fire. Jeremy could see that the monster was awake. Its eyes glared with hatred.

At first Jeremy thought that it was getting ready to attack him, but then he realised that it was looking around for a way to escape. Just as it was about to fly into the air and away, Jeremy had a sudden thought – the creature had attacked Charlotte. Maybe the only way to cure her was through the help of that same creature. As the idea passed through his mind his foot moved onto the monster's wing, trapping it so that it could not fly away. It snarled and screeched, and tried to snap at him, but it could not quite reach.

Then a grating voice came from the creature's beak. "Let me go! Let me go!" the voice said. "The fire will be upon me in a moment and I shall be destroyed. Let me fly away. I promise that I shall never harm any living creature again."

Jeremy thought quickly, and then replied, "I'll free you if you put right the harm you've done to my sister. What did you do to make her so mindless? "

The creature looked wildly about. There was very little time left before the blue fire touched its outstretched wing. Madly it gabbled its reply to Jeremy: "I eat living minds."

"You horrible monster!" Jeremy shouted. His voice was loud and harsh with anger. "You must give Charlotte's mind back, if you don't you'll die in the blue fire like the others did."

To Jeremy's horror, the creature turned its head away and snarled.

"I won't help," its voice grated. "Even if I am swallowed by the fire, it will not help you. Your sister will never be able to think again."

The blue flames touched the tip of the great, leathery wing. The monster screamed again and again as the fire crawled all over it, bursting into a thousand white-hot holes.

"I will help you," it screamed. "Take the fire away, I will do anything you ask. I will help. "

But it was too late. With a blinding, blue flash the whole of its body was crossed, backwards and forwards with lines of jagged light. With a final great screech of pain and rage, it was blasted into dust, which rose up into the air and floated away. As it faded from sight, so did the blue fire.

Jeremy was tired and weary. He looked at Charlotte standing there so silent and unaware. For a moment he leaned back against the rocky wall and closed his eyes. Almost instantly he opened them again as he heard a faint noise.

"Surely there are no more of the mind-stealers left," he said to Twitch, looking around. The noise came again, not from over his head, but from near where Charlotte was standing.

"Listen," he said to Twitch. "That sounded just like a yawn." He turned and peered through the gloom towards Charlotte. He was just in time to see her eyes flicker. As if waking from a deep sleep, she yawned again.

"What on earth's happened?" she asked as she rubbed her eyes.

"You're awake!" Jeremy shouted, delighted. As they continued down the pathway, he told Charlotte all that had happened.

When they approached the bright, shining light they saw that it came from an open doorway. Just a few more steps and they had left the dark passageway behind.

"Look at that!" Jeremy exclaimed.

In front of them was an enormous golden room. It was so wide that they could not see across to the far side. Golden light shimmered and flashed over the walls, floor and roof. There was music and laughter coming from a crowd of people, pressing around them, talking and shouting in excitement.

But the children did not spend too much time looking around. Their attention was quickly drawn to the centre of the marvellous room. A great golden throne floated just above the floor. Seated in it was a figure of gold, a giant, dressed in blue clothes. It was hard to see him clearly because the air surrounding him flashed and sparkled, dazzling the children's eyes. But they could see that his face was kind, and there was a smile in his eyes.

More and more people began to notice Jeremy and Charlotte. Gradually, the room became silent, and slowly the people moved back, forming a path that led to the Golden Giant.

"Maybe we should go up to his throne," Charlotte whispered.

"Yes, I think so," Jeremy answered.

As they approached, they heard the giant's low, gentle voice.

"Do not be afraid, my children," he told them. "I am the Comet Blazer, and all these people are my friends and helpers. We love to be happy and friendly, and we harm no one."

The Comet Blazer then told the children a sad story.

One night, not knowing that the Mind Stealers were near, he and all of his friends were celebrating the evening of the shooting stars. They were caught completely by surprise when the Mind Stealers attacked, and most of his friends had their minds taken before they had a chance to run. For many years they forgot how to play, or dance, or laugh or sing. Worse still, they were unable to look after their jobs of brightening the night sky, so the skies became dark and cold, with never the silvery trail of a shooting star, nor the wondrous blaze of a comet.

"Then," the Comet Blazer said. "You fought the mind stealers and destroyed them all. You set free all of the minds that had been taken. Thank you very much. The night sky will be beautiful again." The Comet Blazer paused and smiled at the children. "Now, look carefully."

The giant stretched his arm, and pointed a finger. From its very tip, a glitter of gold and silver sparks spun and tumbled and joined together to form a misty ball of glowing fire. It floated down to where the children were standing. Just in front of them, it hovered in the air. Charlotte reached out towards it, gasping with delight as it settled gently into her outstretched hands. It felt soft and warm. Then it started to spin again, faster and faster, and the gold and silver sparks flew off in all directions. Faster still, and the shower of sparks was like a small fountain, forming a fiery outline around Charlotte's face and shoulders.

Then, as suddenly as it had started, the fiery stream vanished. In place of the ball of fire, laying in Charlotte's hand, was a tiny, jewelled key.

There was a noise like thunder, and a great white light shone. The children's eyes were dazzled, and for a moment they couldn't see anything. Then the light was gone, and with it, the great golden room, the Comet Blazer and the crowds of happy people.

Jeremy, Charlotte and Twitch found themselves alone in total darkness.

UNDERGROUND WORLD

The darkness was complete. Charlotte reached out in front of her and her fingers touched wet fur. "Is that you, Twitch?" she whispered.

"Meow," was the reply.

"Jeremy, where are you?" Charlotte asked.

There was a shuffling noise just ahead and a voice answered through the gloom. "I'm here. I've just bumped my head on the roof. It's very low, so be careful!"

"Come over here to us, Jeremy. We must keep together in this darkness."

"I wonder where we are," Jeremy said.

They both outstretched their arms and started to explore in the darkness.

"We seem to be in a tunnel, a narrow tunnel," said Charlotte.

"Where's this drip-dripping sound coming from?" Jeremy wondered.

"I don't know. It must be water dripping from somewhere." The ground below them was wet and very muddy, squelching underfoot.

"Meow! Yuk! I don't like it," said Twitch.

"I wonder how we got here," murmured Charlotte.

"The same way as always, of course," Jeremy replied. "It is the magic of the other keys drawing us onwards."

"In that case," Charlotte said slowly, "there must be a real reason for us to have been brought here. I guess we'll find some little creatures in trouble, who need our help. That means that the next key is here too."

Jeremy nodded thoughtfully, thinking to himself that creatures in trouble meant more problems, but he did not say anything. "Which way shall we go," he asked. In the darkness all directions appeared to be the same.

Charlotte considered carefully before replying. "I can't see any light at all, but I can feel a faint current of air blowing in my face. Can you feel the air moving?"

"Oh, yes," Jeremy replied.

"Well," Charlotte continued, "it must be blowing from somewhere outside, so that's the way for us to go."

They set off carefully through the darkness. It became more and more uncomfortable as water fell on them from the roof. Mud clogged their shoes and soaked through to their feet. Every now and then there was a cry as a head banged against an extra low part of the rocky roof. As they continued along the way, the roof began to get lower so that they had to stoop, and then crouch. The sides of the tunnel became closer and closer.

It was beginning to get almost too low and narrow to move.

"Maybe we're walking into a dead end," Jeremy said.

"No, we can't be," Charlotte denied. "If we were, the air wouldn't be blowing into my face."

Soon she was proven right. As they turned yet another bend, a glimmer of light flickered ahead of them. They saw that they were on the side of a vast cave, which seemed to be miles and miles wide, and stretched upwards into an enormous gloomy haze. The light seemed to come from bluey-green, glass globes on the right hand wall of the cave.

"Stop," whispered Charlotte to the others, and for a time they all halted, still just inside the tunnel and hidden round a small bend.

"Keep absolutely quiet," Charlotte continued. "I'm sure that I heard something not far ahead."

She edged forward, peeping round the corner of the bend, but then she couldn't help giving a small cry of surprise. In front of her was an amazing and frightening sight. Jeremy rushed to her side.

The tunnel ended on a rocky ledge, a few metres up on the wall of the cave. Charlotte and Jeremy had a complete view of everything that was going on. There were thousands of white worm-like creatures moving in all directions, some very slowly, some with great speed. They were all carrying heavy loads which they were emptying down a great hole not far from where the children stood. The wind that the children felt was coming from the rather heavy breathing of these creatures. The whole time there was a soft clicking noise.

"Where does the noise come from?" Charlotte asked.

"It must come from the claws that stick out of their heads," Jeremy guessed.

"I don't like the look of those," groaned Charlotte.

" I wonder if they are dangerous," Jeremy said.

It was not long before his question was answered. As they watched, the children saw a large ant fall from the rocks nearby and tumble down among the worms. In a flash it was seized in the grip of the claws of the nearest worm, torn to pieces and pushed into a round, toothless mouth. Immediately, the other worm creatures started to fight and struggle, trying to steal the ant away. They slashed and cut, hacking at one another with their wicked claws. In a very short time the ground was littered with dead worms. Then, one of the monsters rushed forward to eat the dead creatures scattered around. Soon there was not a trace of the struggle left.

"That's horrible!" said both Charlotte and Jeremy.

"We must find a way out of this cave," Charlotte said.

They looked everywhere, up and down, to the sides and across, but there were only two openings into the cave: one was the tunnel entrance through which they had just crawled, and the other . . . Well, it was not worth thinking about it. It was down the hole, in the cave floor, in the middle of all the horrid worms.

"I don't want to go back into the tunnel," Charlotte said. "There must be another way. The ant came from somewhere, and so do the worms."

Jeremy was quiet, watching the worms carefully. He believed that he had seen some of them climb over the edge of the hole. A brighter, yellow light shone from there. Yes, he was right. Some worms were going down, some were coming up.

"Look at that light," he said to Charlotte and explained what he had found out.

"But how on earth can we get across without getting caught?"

"First we must be sure that we can get down the hole safely. It might be very deep and steep for us to climb down," said Jeremy.

"I'm going to have a look. I'll wear the Cloak of Invisibility, so the worms won't see me," replied Charlotte.

Hugging Twitch tightly, Jeremy waited, crouching on the ground, just inside the tunnel's entrance. He watched as Charlotte prepared for the dangerous trip across the floor of the cave.

It was always a strange thing, to see Charlotte putting on the Cloak of Invisibility. First she searched through the haversack, took out the Cloak and shook the creases out. Then, as she slipped it over her shoulders, and let the bottom of it fall to her feet, she disappeared.

Inside the Cloak, Charlotte saw Jeremy's eyes blink as she disappeared. It was strange to see Jeremy and Twitch staring right through the place where she stood, as if she did not exist. She started her exploration. The hole in the cave's floor seemed a long way off as she crept slowly forward, dodging the worms as they crawled around.

From close by, they looked even more horrible than before. Charlotte could tell by the way their heads kept turning in her direction that, although they could not see her, they could sense that she was near. Maybe they could smell her.

The hole in the middle of the cave had seemed a long way away when she started off, but it was not. Almost before she knew it, she drew near. As she did so, her nose was filled with the most nauseating smell imaginable. The closer she got, the stronger the smell became until, at the very edge of the hole, she could hardly bear it. Her stomach heaved and a strong feeling of sickness came over her.

Trying to ignore the stench, she leaned over the side and looked down. It was a long way down. The first thing she saw was that, down there, was another huge cave – even vaster than the one she was in. It was almost like another world, with rivers and mountains, grass and trees. It was brightly lit, with the light coming from great clusters of purple-coloured toadstools which grew thickly everywhere – on the walls, on the ground and all over the roof. They glowed like a million half-lit candles.

On the ground were hundreds and hundreds of ants – just like the one which had been torn to pieces by the worms. They were covered with orange fur. They rushed about in every direction in a seemingly mindless way. But it was soon plain to Charlotte that their frantic activity was far from being mindless. They were all carrying heavy loads of the horrible, rotted material that was being pushed over the edge by the worms.

Charlotte felt most curious. What exactly was being thrown down by the worms? She watched carefully as the next group of the creatures approached. She moved over to stand near them as they started to toss their loads into the hole. She could hardly believe her eyes when she saw the strange assortment of rubbish they were carrying. Piles of old roots and leaves, dead insects, twigs, grass – even a dead frog. All of it seemed to be mouldy and decaying – no wonder there was such a terrible smell.

Then her eyes were attracted to a small opening in the side of the cave below. There was nothing going or coming from it. It seemed strange, in view of the crowds of ants around. The opening did seem to be the safest direction to take.

Charlotte thought hard, trying to form a plan which would bring them all through without harm.

"If only the Cloak of Invisibility were big enough to cover us all," she said to herself.

She rose to her feet and started to make her way back to the others. All the time she tried to think of a plan. Just as she reached Jeremy and Twitch, the answer came to her like a flash of light. She would have to make two journeys, first with the cloak hiding herself and Jeremy, then hiding herself and Twitch."

"Jeremy," she whispered – and he nearly jumped out of his skin, for he had no idea that she was near. "Come with me," she said to him. "Twitch, you stay here. I'll soon come back for you."

Quietly and secretly, the children tiptoed between the giant worms, and reached the edge of the hole. It did not take them long to find a steep slope of loose rocks which led dangerously to the bottom. With enormous caution they climbed downwards, finding their path very hard and painful as the sharp rocks dug into their feet and ankles. At the steepest parts they had to crawl, hurting their knees. After what seemed like hours they reached the bottom.

Then, together, they ran, as fast as they could between the busy ants and into the small entrance which Charlotte had spotted before. The ants had taken no notice of them at all.

"Stay here," Charlotte said to Jeremy, pointing at a big, old tree root. "I'm going back for Twitch." As she rose to her feet to go, she noticed another tunnel leading into the darkness behind where Jeremy sat, but she had no time to look further. She was anxious to go and rescue Twitch.

All seemed to be going to plan, when disaster struck. Charlotte's foot slipped on a loose stone, the cloak caught on a jagged rock and, before she could do anything, it was torn from her shoulders. At once she was visible to all the monstrous worms. Their evil claws clicked deafeningly as they fastened their eyes upon her.

Closer and closer they crawled. Charlotte was so frightened she could not move. Now she could see right down into their hungry red mouths, dripping with green slime. She shivered in panic as she looked into the small, red eyes, round and staring at the thought of the meal she would make.

Then, the nearest one reached out with its claws. It could almost touch her. Frantically, she stretched out her hand towards the Cloak, which lay on the ground beside her. With a gasp of dismay, she found that it was just out of her reach. As she stretched further she fell on the loose stones, tumbling sideways and backwards.

As she fell her fingers closed on a large, jagged rock. With all her strength she lifted it high, and brought it crashing down on the head of the worm that was almost upon her. The creature fell, rolling over and over. Charlotte had gained a few precious moments of time, which enabled her to reach out again towards the cloak.

This time her outstretched hand closed over the edge of the cloak. Quickly, she threw it over her shoulders and instantly disappeared from the worms' sight.

Everything, then seemed to go mad. The worms became wild with rage and disappointment at the thought of losing such a tasty meal. They stood up high in the air on their tails, searching for her, their great white bodies looking like monstrous ghosts. As they crashed back to the ground, their anger and fury turned into hate and madness, and everywhere they turned fiercely on one another, slashing and killing with their dreadful claws.

Through all this tearing, roaring, murderous battle, Charlotte dashed back to Twitch. He was sitting and watching the worms with great anxiety. He realised that all the raging fighting must have somehow been caused by Charlotte and he knew that she must be somewhere near. He was not surprised, therefore, when out of nowhere, hands reached for him, and he found himself tucked under her arm. But he did shut his eyes when, within the shelter of the Cloak, she made her way back between the vicious monsters.

Although he was well hidden, Jeremy could hear the terrible noise and he wondered what was happening above. The more dreadful the noise became, the more he worried over Charlotte and Twitch. Even the furry ants stopped working as they too, listened to the terrible struggle that was going on above their heads.

The whole vast cave shook and trembled as the Worms heaved their huge bodies into the air, and thundered to the ground. The rocks started to shake and split under the impact. Great cracks began to appear on the walls and roof, and enormous slabs of rock started to break away and fall to the ground, raising thick clouds of dust. The thrashing bodies of the worms could be seen dimly, as if in a nightmare.

With a last unbelieving look around her, Charlotte dashed down the slope, half sliding, half rolling. She reached the bottom only just in time. A second later there was an ear-splitting roar. A great shower of rocks and dust rose into the air and smashed down around her. The upper cave collapsed, burying the dreadful worms forever. A few small stones rolled down, the choking grey dust settled and an eerie silence filled the air.

The ants stood around, unmoving, staring at the place – now blocked with rocks – from where they had collected their heavy loads. They seemed unable to understand that the supply of rotting material had stopped.

It was easy for Charlotte to run between them, anxious to find Jeremy. She called out to him, "Jeremy!"

There was no reply, even when she called again, more loudly. She looked around, but found no trace of him.

There were many thick, strong roots growing down from the roof overhead, stretching down from a great tree above-ground. They looked exactly like the bars of a cage. In a way, that is exactly what they turned out to be. Charlotte turned round to leave the cave, but she found that the roots had, as if by magic, suddenly grown down behind her, surrounding her on every side.

It was then that she heard Jeremy calling, "Here!" Peering through the dim light, in the direction of the sound, she finally saw him.

Jeremy, too was trapped by the roots, but Twitch was free – he was small enough to slip between the root-bars, and when he saw Charlotte he started to run frantically backwards and forwards.

Except for a furry ant, there were no other creatures about. "I bet they don't come here because it's too dangerous," Charlotte said to herself. "I should've thought of that."

While she was saying that, she noticed that Twitch had stopped running. Twitch and the furry ant were staring silently at one another. Suddenly Twitch shook himself and made an odd noise – half like a purr, half like a growl. The ant scurried away, his orange fur gleaming in the purplish light.

"What was all that about?" Charlotte asked.

"The ant and I are able to read each other's thoughts. The ant told me that they are all slaves to an enormous beetle – easily as large as Jeremy and bright golden in colour. The beetle has no claws or sharp teeth – instead, it uses electricity as a weapon to fight and kill, and to punish any ant that does not work hard enough."

"What about the worms?" Charlotte asked.

"Even the worms were slaves," Twitch replied. "They were responsible for finding food for the beetles. The ants were responsible for storing it in special caves along the cliff edge."

"I see," Charlotte said, still amazed.

"All the beetles are furious now because the worms were destroyed, and they know that we caused it."

"Perhaps the ants won't tell the beetles about where we are hiding," said Jeremy hopefully.

But Twitch shook his head. "The ant is too frightened of the Beetles," he spoke gloomily. "He'll certainly tell them we are here."

"We must get away from here before they find us," Charlotte said.

86

Twitch sat up, curling his tail around him. "True," he said, but that was all. He shut his eyes and seemed to go to sleep.

Charlotte eyed the cat in annoyance. If she had been able to get close to him, she would have given his tail a hard pull. She shook the roots which held her, again and again, but she could not move them even a few centimetres, they were so thick and solid.

"We can't get out," she said sadly.

"There must be a way," Jeremy said. Then they both went quiet.

Time passed. Twitch woke up, and started pacing up and down between the two caged children. Jeremy sat with his eyes shut, hands still firmly grasping the unmoving roots. Charlotte lay on her back with her arm across her face, trying desperately to think of a plan to escape.

Therefore neither saw the small movement overhead. It was not until there was a slight scrabbling noise that Jeremy looked up.

"Charlotte, look!" he cried out, pointing upwards. There, tumbling down from a hole in the roof, was a small brown animal, half rabbit, half squirrel. As the creature dropped to the ground, it stared at the children in great surprise. While it did so, several more fell from the roof and formed a circle around Jeremy and Charlotte. At last one of the animals spoke, in a rusty, creaky voice.

"You are in a fix! You have been caught by the roots of a giant tree which grows high up into the sunshine. Our homes are in its branches, and we come down here to search for food."

"You do?" Charlotte said, to make conversation.

"Yes, we take it from the ants, you see? They are so stupid that they don't even realise that we're taking it."

"Who are you?" Charlotte asked. At once the small creatures bounced over to her.

"We are bunny hoppers, of course," one of them replied.

The children could easily understand how they had got their name. Instead of walking, the funny little creatures moved along by bouncing into the air. All the time they made funny little twittering noises.

"The tree must have thought you were seedlings. Its seeds are planted deep in these caves, and when they sprout they are protected by a barrier of roots. Don't worry, when it thinks you are the right size, and can look after yourselves properly, the tree will pull its roots away, and release you."

Charlotte's hopes rose a great deal when she heard this.

"Perhaps things aren't going to be so bad after all," Jeremy said.

"But how long is that likely to be?" Charlotte asked anxiously.

The bunny hopper paused and thought hard, its head on one side. Then, it smiled and replied cheerfully, "Oh, not long. Only about ten years, I expect."

Charlotte sat down with a bump. "Ten years!" she said, thoroughly alarmed. "Ten years! We can't live that long like this!" What can we do?"

The bunny hopper thought hard again, and then frowned. "Well," it replied, "when one of us gets caught, we nibble at the roots. The tree certainly does not like that at all, and it soon lets us go."

"That isn't much good to us," Charlotte replied. "we haven't got long, sharp teeth to nibble the roots with," but as she said so, the bunny hoppers were gone! They bounced away down the track, and their twittering voices gradually faded into the distance.

Feeling really exhausted, Jeremy went to sleep. Meanwhile, Charlotte leaned back on the haversack and closed her eyes. She really needed to think again and try to find a way out, but she couldn't get into a comfortable position. Something sharp was digging into her back, scratching her shoulder each time she moved. Although she tried to ignore it, the discomfort continued. She sat up and put the haversack on her knee so that she could open it and look for the cause.

At first there seemed to be no reason, but as Charlotte looked more closely she found it. "Aha! That's it!" she shouted.

"That's what?" Jeremy cried in alarm.

"A sharp thorn caught in the haversack has been hurting my back."

"A thorn?"

"Yes, strange. I guess it must've come from the bushes where we tumbled over and over, near the Golden Castle, remember?" She felt carefully around the haversack. She tried to loosen the thorn, but even though she tugged and tugged, it wouldn't move. It was far bigger and stronger than she'd thought. Her fingers grew sore from trying to get a grip on the sharp edge. She put all her strength into one final attempt and, suddenly, the thorn came free. It happened so unexpectedly that she fell head over heels backwards.

"Are you alright?" Jeremy asked.

"Yes," she said. "Look at this thorn."

Jeremy pressed his face against the roots to try see what Charlotte had in her hands. "Thorn? I thought it was a big nail," he said.

Charlotte tried to scratch one of the roots with it. "Perhaps it'll work like the bunny hoppers' teeth," she called out excitedly. But, try as she might, the roots were so hard that the thorn made not the slightest impression.

Charlotte felt very disappointed.

"I know," Jeremy said. "You need something to hammer it in." "Take off your shoe, that should do the trick."

Charlotte pulled off one of her shoes. Using the heel, and striking with all her strength, she slowly knocked the thorn deep into the side of the largest root.

The result was explosively fantastic. There was a sound like the crack of a whip, and the roots all around started to quiver. The ground under each root began to split and a low thundery noise filled the air. The whole cave trembled. With lightning speed the roots around Charlotte tore themselves out from the ground and whipped up over her head, finally disappearing high into the roof.

Everything then became still and silent.

"I'm free!" Charlotte said.

"Give me a hand, then" Jeremy said, but the thorn that had helped her escape was now gone. Charlotte rummaged through the haversack for another thorn, but there wasn't any.

"There must be something else," she said. "Wait! What's this?" At the bottom of the bottle which had contained the Water of Protection, three tiny drops could be seen, gleaming in the strange purple light. With the greatest care Charlotte unscrewed the cap, and with her fingers crossed for luck, she scattered the three tiny droplets onto three of the roots which still held Jeremy captive, but nothing happened. Not the slightest movement disturbed the thick root-bars.

"Why, oh why doesn't the magic water work?" she thought sadly as the drops of water lay there on the roots, shining brightly.

But then, suddenly there was a small puff of steam. A thread of smoke rose into the air and drifted downwards, seeming to soak into the wood. At once the roots started to twist and bend, a little at first, then more and more violently. As they did so they began to swell, becoming fatter and fatter. The gaps between the roots began to change. First they became narrower, then wider, narrower, wider, narrower, wider, over and over again.

This was Jeremy's chance! At exactly the right moment, when the gaps between the roots were at their widest, Charlotte reached through and, as Jeremy jumped, she pulled as hard as she could. The next moment he was free.

They rolled over and over, to the far side of the cave, laughing and shouting with happiness at having escaped. Twitch was still sitting and staring at the wildly waving roots.

"Twitch, Twitch, come over here," Charlotte called out to him.

The cat bounded over to join them, and they all moved away from the roots towards the entrance of the second tunnel Charlotte had seen before. It went downwards gently. When the three saw that they were safe, they turned to see what was happening behind them.

The roots now seemed to have gone quite mad. Banging and thrashing, they seemed to be completely out of control, and earth and stones from the roof crashed down in every direction. From all over the cave the bunny hoppers bounced, twittering with fright. In one panic-stricken rush they dashed to the entrance hole and vanished into the world above.

The roots started to burst. The tunnel roof began to split and crack. Rocks, stones and dust started to pour down. With a roar like thunder the whole cave collapsed behind the children's backs.

"Come on!" shouted Charlotte. "There's only one way to go!"

The three set off down the slope of the new tunnel.

The way was easy. Wide and brightly lit from the toadstools, the ground was smooth. They walked on and on for a long time.

Then, quite suddenly, something appeared in front of them, making them stop. It was weird collection of flashing lights of many colours. Odd shadows flickered on the roof and walls. There was a small hump on the pathway which prevented them from seeing any further along the tunnel.

"Where do these lights come from?" Jeremy asked.

"I don't know," Charlotte replied. "Stay here. I'll go and see over the hump."

Very quietly and slowly she made her way up the pathway and peered over the rocky hill.

"Oh!" she gasped.

"What is it?" Jeremy asked anxiously.

"The golden beetles!" Charlotte replied in a loud whisper. "There's another cave, and it's full of them."

Jeremy and Twitch ran to her and saw the scene for themselves. The beetles' golden bodies flashed and gleamed as they crawled and flew around. Whenever they moved, brilliant flashes of many-coloured lights came from their wings and legs.

"Look," Jeremy whispered. "There are the ants."

The beetles were controlling long lines of furry ants. All about them, were high rocky cliffs. On every cliff were hundreds of exactly round holes. The heavily laden ants were struggling up towards the holes along narrow tracks cut into the rocky walls.

"The smell is terrible," Jeremy commented. "It's stronger than before."

"This must be where the beetles store their food," Charlotte said, hand over her mouth and nose, as the stench was so bad.

An ant was going very slowly and finally stopped. It was immediately punished by a flash of blue beetle-electricity. An especially cruel beetle came along. Instead of a blue flash, it fired an ugly red one. The poor ant fell over onto its back, its small legs waving in the air. It then slowly turned black and, in a few seconds dissolved into a small heap of grey dust. The beetle gave a kind of laugh and kicked the dust into the air.

"We must do something about it," Jeremy said.

"I wonder what we could use from the haversack," Charlotte added.

Jeremy started to look carefully around the immense cavern. It was then that he noticed, high on the cliff, a silvery, rippling movement. Try as he might, he could not imagine what it might be. "Can you see that?" he pointed.

Charlotte and Twitch looked hard and long at the shining,

moving object. It was Twitch who, at last, spoke thoughtfully. "I do believe that it must be a pool of water, high up at the top of the cliff, trapped by that long, flat rock."

Jeremy laughed. "It can't be!" he said. "Where could it have come from then? We are underground – there's no rain here!"

But Charlotte interrupted. "You are right, Twitch. It probably comes from the hundreds of drips of water that keep falling from the roof."

Jeremy said nothing, but he wasn't sulking. On his face was a look of quiet excitement. In a sudden rush, he started to speak.

"I've got it, Charlotte. I know how we can do it. Water! Electricity! Two terribly dangerous things when you put them together. There's a terrific lot of water, up there, and the beetles are full of electricity. Surely we can use these two things to give the beetles a few shocks?"

"But the water is so high up, and the beetles are a long way below," Charlotte said.

"Let's climb up," Jeremy suggested. They started to climb along a narrow path along the side of the cliff. Then they came to another, smaller, path that seemed to lead directly to the water.

The little pathway was so tightly packed with the ants, one behind the other that, for a while, there was no way that the children could get onto it. At last, there came a gap where, in front of them one of the heavily laden ants had stumbled and fallen. Seizing their chance, they slipped in between two of the little creatures and, holding their noses against the terrible smell, they began to climb the path up the cliff.

Steeper and steeper, higher and higher they went. Now it was almost like a ladder, and neither of the children dared to look down. Their legs were aching, and they were puffing and panting, when at last they could see, over to their side, the gleam and glint of water.

Charlotte and Jeremy were very much relieved to leave the crowded path, even though they now had to scramble dangerously across the cliff side, trying to find footholds wherever they could.

As they made their way across the loose rocks, suddenly, Jeremy slipped. His feet kicked against a large, round boulder and sent it smashing and tumbling down the cliff side. The sound seemed to crash and echo, filling the great cave with noise. At once, the air above the children's heads was crowded with the evil beetles, who zoomed and buzzed with horrible temper as they saw the rocks falling.

In two seconds the furious beetles were on the attack, firing huge numbers of the red-hot sparks, which hit the ground, and bounced off the rocks, showering around the children's heads.

Twitch jumped and scrambled all over the place, dodging the sparks. To Charlotte's and Jeremy's surprise, Twitch was actually enjoying himself. Twitch's clever, fast jumps drove the beetles madder and madder. They began to lose control over their sparks and started to crash into each other in mid flight.

The children didn't waste any time. Soon they were by the waterside and found that the pond was far larger than they had imagined. It was more like a small lake! And it was exactly above the place where most of the beetles were gathered on the ground below. As the children examined the deep water, they saw that there was just one great rock which had made a dam. That was the only rock that stopped the water from flooding downwards.

"We have to shift that rock," said Charlotte. "Any ideas?"

Jeremy's brains refused to work. The rock was as big as several houses and he could see no way at all of being able to shift it. If only they had some dynamite. As he stood thinking, standing with his hands in his pockets, his fingers touched the carving given by the Wood Gnome – it had been there ever since he had used it to fight off the mind stealers.

"The gnome!" he said to Charlotte.

Holding the little wooden object in front of him, he touched the magic star. Closing his eyes, he wished hard. As had happened before, there seemed to be no response at first, but suddenly the carving moved in his hand, twisting around until it pointed directly at the huge rock. Then it began to tremble and shake, until it became almost too hard to hold.

At that point a pale greenish light, like a small globe, floated lazily up from it and hovered in the air. Gently, and without haste, the shining globe drifted across towards the great rock and lightly settled down upon it. Small glowing fingers of green fire began to spread, until the entire rock was covered by a network of spidery

93

sparks. Then this web of light began to grow brighter, twisting and curling like the arms of an octopus and the rock started to shiver and shake along its whole massive length. As it did so, there was a low, growling noise like distant thunder. With an ear-splitting sound, thousands of cracks appeared in its sides. Finally, with a terrible, frightening crash and a blinding flash of green light, the rock was gone.

With a rushing roar the water started to pour over the edge of the cliff. It ran down towards the valley below, carrying mud, rocks and huge boulders with it.

There was no way the beetles could escape the deluge. It was a terrifying sight to see. As the water sprayed over the electric beetles, there was a blinding sea of green flashes. Then they began to explode in sheets of green and yellow fire. The noise was terrific.

The water spread and spread, and soon there were so many of the cruel creatures caught by it, that the air in every direction was filled with smoke. There were flashes of light everywhere, and the cave became as bright as day.

A strange mixture of smells began to rise. Electricity, steam and smoke mingled with the ever present odour of rotting food.

As Jeremy and Charlotte felt that their eyes, ears and noses could stand no more, it all came to a stop. In the silence that followed, the smoke and fumes drifted away. Now, nothing moved except for an odd wisp of steam, here and there, and a few small stones that rolled quietly down the rocky slope.

Jeremy moved close to the cliff edge, and looked around. "Amazing," he said. "The beetles have all been destroyed!"

"Look," Charlotte said. "There's something moving down there."

Then they saw the ants scattered around in the places where they had crouched down in terror when their world had started to explode.

"Don't be frightened," Charlotte called, "You're free now."

Slowly the bad smell disappeared as the rotting food was swept away by the water. The purple toadstools, which had given such a sickly light, had been swept away too. With them gone, there was now a silvery gleam reflecting from every rock. It lit the great cavern with a soft pearly light.

As Jeremy and Charlotte carefully picked their way down the steep path the furry ants gathered around them. Then, as the children reached the bottom, they heard a murmur, becoming louder and louder and across the crowds of ants there was a bustling movement: a strange carriage was coming towards them. It was made of silvery, dried grasses and ferns. Sitting upon it was an old ant, its orange fur turning white with age. Gently the carriage came to a rest and the buzz from the ants faded away.

The old ant looked at Jeremy and Charlotte for a while. In a whispering, dry voice it began to speak, so quietly that it was difficult to hear.

"We have been waiting a long time for you to come," the old ant said. "We knew that one day you would be here to free us. The books have always promised that. The promise has been kept, and the books tell me that I must take you to the crystal of ice. I cannot tell you why, for I am not allowed to know. All I do know is that, somewhere within the crystal, there is something which you are seeking."

The old ant signalled to the others, and the carriage was lifted from the ground, carried on the backs of a dozen proud looking ants. it moved slowly towards the sides of the cliffs.

"Where can it be going?" puzzled Charlotte, for there appeared to be no way forward, but almost as she spoke, a pale light shimmered on the rocky wall. A great door swung noiselessly open, leading the way into a wide, brightly-lit tunnel, sparkling with gleams of white fire. Only a second before there had been no trace of the door at all. Then the ants and everything else faded away in a pink light.

As if from a great distance they heard the dry voice of the old ant. "Go forward, my friends," it urged them. "Go forward. No harm will come to you. We can come no further. Farewell. You will always be remembered with love."

The voice faded. The children knew that the ants and their underground world had gone forever.

"Come on Twitch," said Jeremy. "Okay, Charlotte?"

Charlotte nodded.

The three travellers walked through the thick pink mist. It was a strange feeling, walking without being able to see a thing. But they did not feel the slightest bit afraid – only very excited at what might lay ahead.

It was not many moments before they saw a glowing shape, dimly shining through the mist. As they drew near they could see that it looked like a gigantic diamond, made of glittering ice. The closer they approached, the colder it became until the children could hardly feel their arms or legs, and their breath drifted in puffs of white into the glowing air. As if in a dream, they were drawn forward.

At last, the children were standing immediately before the cold, shimmering crystal.

From nowhere, a voice spoke. "Reach out, and touch the crystal," it commanded.

Slowly, Charlotte's hand reached towards the icy diamond. Jeremy held his breath as he watched, hugging Twitch close to his chest.

Charlotte's outstretched fingers gently touched the great crystal. As they did so, there was a soft chime, as if made by a lonely silver bell. In an instance the crystal shattered into a million snowflakes, which twisted and turned in a thousand beautiful shapes until they drifted away in every direction.

The pink mist faded and the air became clear. A small, sparkling table of ice stood where the great crystal had been. Upon the table lay a blue, velvety box.

Charlotte lifted the box, holding it carefully in her hand before daring to open the lid. Inside was a small, plain key. It looked ordinary and was made of wood. However, to Jeremy and Charlotte it was worth a thousand diamonds.

MACHINE CHILDREN

At last the children tore their attention away from their plain, but marvellous key. When they looked around they were taken by surprise to find that they were now in a wide, green field, filled with birds and flowers. Gone was the pink mist, the tunnel, and the great cavern. The sun shone from a cloudless blue sky.

"Maybe we're back in Home World," Charlotte said, gazing around.

"Maybe," said Jeremy. But he was more interested in a dark blue, star-shaped little flower growing among the grass. He reached out to pick it and . . . "Ouch!" he screamed. On his finger was a large, angry-looking blister. When he looked at the beautiful little flower, it had changed colour to a fierce red.

"This is *not* Home World," Charlotte said.

"Look," said Jeremy, pointing at the flower again. "It's changing back to blue again." Soon it looked exactly as it had before.

"I wonder if all the flowers are so dangerous," Charlotte said to Jeremy. She gently touched the petals of a yellow flower which reminded her of the buttercups which grew back on Home World. "Ouch!" It was her turn to jump up in pain. On her fingertip there was a small spot of blood. To her horror, a small mouth filled with tiny teeth had appeared on the flower when she touched it. The mouth disappeared the instant she took her finger away, leaving the small flower looking sweet and innocent once more.

Together the children examined the flowers which covered the grass, touching them gently with some long twigs. Cautiously, Charlotte reached forward and touched a white flower. The petals snapped upright and violently seized the twig, with a thin screeching noise. The twig seemed to come alive in Charlotte's hand, wriggling and twisting in an attempt to escape from the poisonous grip of the white flower.

Charlotte screamed and dropped the twig onto the ground. The children watched in amazement as the horrible flower and the twig-creature struggled fiercely, swaying and crashing about in the grass. The other flowers stabbed and thrust, trying to fasten their teeth into anything that moved within their reach. Soon the whole field was alive with the frenzied thrashing of evil plants.

Over this horrible scene there arose a high, wavering, screeching noise. Whether it came from the twigs or the flowers, the children could not make out. Covering their ears to shut out the noise, they waited and watched.

As quickly as it had started, it all stopped. With a great bending twist, the twig broke away and at once turned back into the quiet, unmoving object that it had been before. The white, daisy-like flower again became the small, dainty bloom that it had first appeared to be. All the movement and noise across the whole field stopped, and again it was just a lazy meadow, half asleep in the warm sunshine.

"Let's get away from here," said Twitch nervously. With enormous care he tip-toed across the grass, glancing suspiciously at the blooms around him. With every step the three travellers took, the flowers opened and closed their mouths, and snapped and clicked their leaves together, in attempts to get at them.

Twitch purred loudly when they got to the other side. They came to a high, grey, stone wall. The stones which formed the wall were huge, and seemed to be very, very old, for they were cracked. Every crack was filled with small, mossy flowers. Most of the wall was heavily overgrown by a thick climbing plant, with small green flowers, and fleshy brown leaves. The climbing plant tumbled over the top of the wall, high above the children's heads. It was so dense in places that it looked like a small forest. Although there was no wind, the leaves twitched and swayed, seeming to reach out towards the children as if trying to clutch at them. Jeremy stood close, quite fascinated by the movement, and moved his hand towards one of the brown leaves.

"Don't touch!" screamed Charlotte. She pulled him back so hard that he rolled over and over, across the horrible flowers, at one moment seeing the small teeth only inches from his face.

"Why did you do that?" Jeremy said angrily. Charlotte took no notice at all, and he went on complaining.

"Shut up, and watch!" she said sharply.

Jeremy's mouth closed in surprise. He saw Charlotte stoop down and pick up a large piece of stone that had fallen from the wall. She threw it towards the climbing plant. As soon as the stone hit the leaves, stems from all over the plant flashed downwards. The strange green flowers bent their heads, catching the stone in mid-air, before it could fall back to the ground. A thick, colourless liquid oozed from the flowers, over the stone. Bubbles of smoke poured upwards. With a snapping, popping noise the stone broke and crumbled into small fragments, which dropped down to the ground. In a few seconds all that was left was a small heap of sand.

Jeremy looked at this in silence. "Sorry," he said. "I promise I won't be so stupid again."

"Well, that's showed us we can't use this way to leave the field," Charlotte said thoughtfully.

"There must be a gate, or a gap, or something," Jeremy said.

"Let's walk beside the wall," Charlotte suggested. "We should find one."

The field was much larger than it had first seemed. As the sun rose higher in the sky, the children began to feel hot and tired. They had been walking beside the wall for a long time, and had found no gate nor gap through which they could pass.

"Oh no!" Charlotte suddenly said. "Just look, Jeremy."

Jeremy looked to where she was pointing at the ground. All he could see was a small pile of brown dust. "Well," he said, "What's so important about that?"

"Can't you see?" Charlotte said impatiently, stamping her foot. "That's where we threw the stone at the climbing plant."

"Is it? We must have walked completely round the field, then." –

"Yes, and we're back where we started. That means that the wall surrounds us entirely."

They looked at each other feeling miserable and angry at the same time.

"Oh don't be such miseries," growled Twitch. "I don't suppose that you've looked properly at all. You really do need me to help you. Come on. We must walk round again, and this time search more carefully."

The cat stalked off, tail straight up in the air, the tip of it, as usual, gently waving. As he picked his way daintily between the flowers, he appeared to be so sure of himself that the children immediately felt much happier.

Half-way round the field they came to one of the trees they had seen before, with reddish-brown leaves. It was there that Charlotte had picked up the twig. But they noticed something different now: the tree top was so high that it reached clear up and over the wall. In a flash, Twitch sprang into the branches and disappeared amongst the glossy leaves. The children sat down on one of the huge roots and waited anxiously for his return. Soon the cat was back, proudly waving to the children.

"What is it, Twitch?" questioned Charlotte.

"Follow me," Twitch said.

Charlotte hesitated and said, "It looks very high."

Jeremy, who had been walking all around the tree, called to her. "It's like a ladder, Charlotte, look." He showed her how the branches grew in exactly the right places to form a safe ladder upwards.

The children started to climb. Soon they were deep within the shady leaves, where Twitch was impatiently waiting.

It was cosy and warm up there. As they moved along the branches, the tree quivered slightly. It seemed to steady then, gently, with its small twigs and leaves whenever they stumbled.

In front of them was a long, very wide, straight branch. The best thing about it was that it stretched high over the top of the wall. As they crossed the top of the wall, the deadly creeping plant rippled and twisted, sending curled branches high into the air, in an attempt to seize them. But Jeremy and Charlotte were out of reach. Soon they dropped lightly to the ground, on the other side at last.

They were cautious this time. After what had happened in the field of deadly flowers they had no intention of moving or touching anything until they were quite sure that it was safe. They saw that they were now in a wide, grassy meadow, which stretched in all directions around them.

Even though they were now becoming used to new surprises, they still shook their heads in wonder, when they saw that the tree, the wall, and every trace of the garden of flowers had disappeared. There was now only the quiet, grassy meadow, silent under the hot sun. There was not a flower in sight.

Everything was hushed and still, with not even the smallest breeze to disturb the glittering, baking heat. In the distance was a tumbled pile of grey rocks, its outline hazy in the hot air. It was in that direction that Jeremy, Charlotte and Twitch decided to walk.

Tramp, tramp, tramp, their feet moved through the grass with a soft swishing noise.

Twitch suddenly stopped, with one paw still in the air, and said, "Sh!"

"What is it now?" asked Jeremy.

Without answering, Twitch bounded on ahead, up to the top of a small hillock, and there he stopped again, with a surprised look on his face. When the children reached his side they realised why. Below them was the most welcome of sights. Bubbling out from the ground was a silvery, splashing stream of water. It crossed the vast meadow like a thread of light against the green of the grass. The children dashed down the slope. In a moment they were paddling their feet in the cool water. For the time being, their tiredness and aching feet were forgotten.

Twitch kept well clear of the water. Again he was the first one to hear a sound. His tail went up in the air.

"What is it, Twitch?" Charlotte asked. Before he answered she heard the noise too. "Listen!" she said.

"What a strange noise," said Jeremy.

It was the sound of pattering feet – not terribly loud. They peered in every direction to try to discover from where it was coming.

"There!" Jeremy exclaimed, pointing at a cloud of dust drifting towards them.

Then they saw what was causing it: an odd little animal with a round, brown body covered with red stripy markings. It bobbled along on short, white legs. Its white head had large, brown eyes. As it saw the children, it cried out in a frightened voice, "Help! Help!" Its great panic-filled eyes gazed at them fearfully.

Both Charlotte and Jeremy stopped.

"Please help me, please," the little creature continued. "The grobbler is after me, I am too tired to run any further."

"Grobbler?" asked Jeremy.

"What's a grobbler?" Charlotte asked. But without waiting for an answer, she took the cloak of invisibility from the haversack and wrapped it around the animal. Almost at once, another, and much larger cloud of dust descended upon the place. As it approached they were very sure that whatever was causing it must be the creature called the grobbler.

The dust cloud was now only yards away, when it spun round in a circle and came to a skidding halt. As the dust drifted away, it revealed a large creature, shaped very much like a wolf. But it had four wicked looking red eyes, and its mouth contained two rows of pointed, yellow teeth. The creature was bigger than both children put together, and it growled fiercely at them as it prepared to attack.

Picking up the haversack, Charlotte swung it round and round her head. "If you come any closer," she warned in a ferocious voice, "I will smash you with this!" She swung the haversack even more wildly, within inches of the creature's face.

The grobbler snarled and growled horribly, but made no attempt to get any closer. While Charlotte continued to swing the haversack, and kept the creature out of reach, Jeremy gathered a small pile of stones. He began to throw the stones at the grobbler and soon Charlotte joined him.

The horrid creature snarled furiously, but backed even further away, pacing round and round in a large circle still waiting for a chance to attack. It looked rather silly when it ducked and dodged to avoid the stones.

Seeing this, Twitch suddenly felt rather brave. Stalking close, with his tail stiff in the air, he let out the most horrible screeching "Meow" that the children had ever heard. Almost exactly at that moment, one of the larger stones hit the grobbler hard on the very top of its nose. The grobbler bellowed and roared in pain and anger. It stood up on its back legs waving its great claws in the air.

Charlotte could feel the little creature shaking and quivering with fright inside the cloak. "Don't panic," she said softly.

The grobbler continued to circle the children. It was boiling with anger and suspicion. Although it could not see the little creature, it could smell it. But it was also too afraid to come any closer. The children carried on pelting the beast with heavy stones.

At last the grobbler gave up. With a final snarl of its yellow teeth it turned and walked stiffly away, turning every now and again to glare at the children from its red, hate-filled eyes.

When Charlotte saw the creature finally disappear into the hazy distance, and was satisfied that it had really gone, she jumped up and down and cried out, "We've beaten it! We've beaten it, Jeremy!"

Then the children removed the cloak of invisibility from the little creature, carefully folding it and placing it back in the haversack.

"What on earth was all that about?" they asked. "And where did you come from?"

"Thank you for saving me," the little creature replied.

Still trembling with fear it continued, "I'm just a Deemy. I live with the other Deemies in the rock houses over there."

He pointed to the great piles of rocks that the children had seen earlier. "The grobblers constantly hunt us, for food, but they rarely catch us. We are quite safe in our rock houses. When we are attacked, we rush back into our homes in the caves, and we pull big stones in after us to block the entrances. The grobblers stay there for a while, then they give up and go away."

Charlotte looked thoughtful. "That all sounds very well," she said. "But how did you get into so much trouble? The rocks are a very long way away, why are you so far from your home?"

The deemy sighed. "Well," the creature said in a small voice, "I'd been fishing and was half asleep when the grobbler attacked. I jumped, and instead of running to the rocks I fell into the river."

Charlotte could not help smiling. The deemy, seeing her smile became quite huffy.

"It's not at all amusing," it squeaked. "How would you like it if you were comfortably dozing, and then suddenly found yourself in the water being chased by a nasty monster?"

"I'm sorry," Charlotte replied, managing to hide another smile. "It must have been really terrifying. Please go on."

"The river was very deep, and fast flowing," the deemy continued, with a suspicious glance at Charlotte's face, "and I was instantly swept away. Round and round, side to side. I didn't know which way was up. I nearly drowned. Finally the water threw me towards the river bank. I scrambled up almost under the feet of the grobbler which you have frightened away."

As the little creature finished speaking, it tugged and pulled at a curiously twisted green stone ring that it wore on its finger-like claw. Having eased it off, the deemy presented the ring to Charlotte.

"Take this charm," the creature said, "and one day it may help you on your way. If you find you need help, hold the stone in your hand and breathe gently upon it. Help will come."

Charlotte took the ring and carefully slipped it onto her little finger, where it fitted perfectly.

"Thank you," she said.

"What sort of help?" Jeremy asked curiously, but his question fell upon deaf ears. The deemy had turned away, and was bounding rapidly, in a zigzag fashion, across the stony grass, back to the safety of its rock home.

"Come on," Charlotte called to Jeremy, who was still staring in fascination as the deemy disappeared. "Come on. We must get on our way."

"Where to?" Jeremy asked.

"They say that every river leads to the sea. Maybe this stream will too."

They walked on and on, passing the rocky homes of the deemies and eventually losing sight of them as they faded into the distance behind. The sun was low down, and the shadows long, with night approaching fast.

"Where are we going to sleep," Jeremy asked between yawns.

"Maybe here," Charlotte replied. The ground was flat and featureless. Even the stones were now gone. There was just the grass, stretching on and on to meet the great half-circle of the horizon.

A small building came into sight, barely visible in the gloom of evening. It was made of the same grey stones as those forming the deemies' homes, and was exactly square. The children tip-toed to the open door, and peered through the dark shadows inside. The one room was empty and bare, and the floor dusty. Cobwebs hung like flags from every wall. It looked as if the room had not been used for many, many years.

"This will make a good place to spend the night," said Charlotte firmly.

"Yes, it's better than out there in the dark, with the grobblers about," Jeremy said.

They had a little to eat, then wrapped their cloaks tightly around themselves and lay on the floor. Twitch, as usual, snuggled as close to Jeremy as possible. Although the ground was hard, they were all comfortable and warm inside the cloaks. They were soon fast asleep.

In the early hours of the morning Charlotte awoke with a strong feeling that something was wrong.

"What was it?," she wondered, "What has woken me like this?"

A little scared in the deep darkness, she peered around, as much as she could. She listened, but there was nothing to be seen, or heard. For two or three minutes she remained sitting up, trying to think why she had been so alarmed. Then it came to her. Nothing to be heard! Charlotte jumped to her feet with a cry of fear. This was what had awakened her – there was no sound of any kind breaking the total silence. But there should have been!

Where was the sound of breathing from Jeremy? Where were the little growling noises that Twitch always made as he slept, when he dreamed about chasing birds and mice? In the darkness Charlotte grew even more agitated. As her eyes became used to the dim light from the stars, she saw that she was alone.

In absolute panic, she ran outside, down to the stream, calling Jeremy's name, over and over again. There was no answer. Only the murmur of the water and the moaning of the wind disturbed the night air.

Charlotte searched everywhere. Around the building, under the trees, amongst the bushes, and even in the water, but there was no trace of Jeremy or Twitch.

"Where could they have gone? And why?" she cried to herself, leaning against a tree.

She slumped to the ground, with her head in her hands, unable to think or to move. She sat there for a long time until, incredibly, she heard a noise behind her. It was coming from inside the building. She dashed inside.

To her amazement she found both Jeremy and Twitch standing there, looking most bewildered.

"Where have you been?" Charlotte shouted, really very angry that they had scared her so much. "What made you go off like that, and frighten me so?"

"I'm sorry," replied Jeremy, "but we didn't do it on purpose. Twitch turned over in his sleep and must have touched something. There was a clicking noise, and suddenly we found ourselves in a huge room, full of machines. There was no one to look after the

106

machines. We stood there, then we heard the "click" again, and here we are, back with you."

"How strange," Charlotte said, "and if that's what happened we must keep close together for the rest of the night, and in a different corner of the room, well away from where you disappeared."

"In the morning, when there is plenty of light," she continued, "We'll explore, and see what we can find."

After all this excitement they had quite some difficulty in getting back to sleep. Charlotte was still shaking a little, after her fright at finding the other two missing. Jeremy and Twitch were full of impatience to get back into the room of machines.

But at last their tiredness returned, and soon the little building was silent except for the deep breathing of the children and the little growls from Twitch.

The bright sunshine pouring through the open doorway awoke them early. They were soon examining the stone wall where Jeremy had heard the strange "click". For a time they could see nothing different. But then Jeremy found a small, grey button. It looked exactly like stone and could hardly be seen against the grey the wall.

"Great!" said Jeremy, and leaned over to press it, but Charlotte quickly slapped his hand away.

"No one's to touch that button yet," she ordered. "First we must all hold hands. We don't want to be separated again, do we?" She took Jeremy's hand who in turn held Twitch's paw. "Are you ready?" With a final look to make sure they were all holding on to one another firmly, Charlotte shut her eyes – and pressed the button.

At first nothing happened. Then three things occurred all at once. There was a "click" exactly as Jeremy had described it. The stone building disappeared, and suddenly the children were standing in the room filled with machines.

The immense machines stretched in all directions of the vast room. All along gleaming white walls were row upon row of windows. Through the windows could be seen more and more of the buildings, and through the windows in those buildings, the children could see line after line, row after row of the same kind of machines which surrounded the spot where they stood.

The machines were shimmering and shining as great wheels spun round and round, silently reflecting the sunlight. As Jeremy and Charlotte drew nearer, they could see faint coloured lights coming and going, floating for a while and then disappearing, before coming back again. There were thousands of the machines, each one with its mysterious, spinning wheels. But despite the non-stop movement everywhere, there was not the faintest sound, and the air seemed silent and deserted.

Charlotte too was silent. She had been examining the machines carefully, and was trying to imagine what they were doing. But they didn't seem to be making anything at all – at least, nothing that she could see. In fact, except for the wheels, there was little to be seen of the machines at all, for they were like small enclosed rooms: black boxes with large black pipes leading to huge storage bins.

"Can you see inside?" Charlotte whispered to Jeremy.

"No, it's too high for me to see over the sides," Jeremy whispered back. "But look over there. There's a strange thing, something like a moving platform."

Charlotte looked and saw a platform stacked high with small boxes. All the time it carried loads and loads of the boxes into yet another building. "It's all very confusing," she said.

"It must be a factory," Jeremy said. "But why is it so quiet?"

They almost felt that they should walk on tip-toe as they crossed the wide floor, into the next room. When they arrived there, they were both lost for words. What the children saw now was startling: an army of small, silver robots was buzzing to and fro. Seemingly undirected, and looking in an absolute muddle, they were frantically collecting the boxes and stacking them into piles. There must have been millions of the boxes, and they were stacked so high that they wobbled and swayed. All the time large numbers of them were falling down and spilling over into the yard surrounding the factory.

The giant piles of boxes covered the floor as far as could be seen, along a seemingly endless hallway. The whole time there was the movement of boxes tumbling and toppling over into the yard below.

Suddenly one of the boxes fell down and landed immediately in front of Jeremy. Before Charlotte could stop him, he reached down and opened it.

"There's nothing in it! Nothing at all!" Jeremy exclaimed.

Charlotte turned completely round, in a circle, looking at the countless numbers of empty boxes, piled one on top of another, in every direction. "What are they for?" she murmured.

She thought for a while, and finally seemed to have found the answer. "I know," she said in a half-whisper.

"What do you know?" Jeremy asked.

"Once there must have been people here, making things, and the robots packed the things into the boxes. Now the people have all gone, and so there is nothing to pack, but the machines don't know, and so they continue to make the boxes, all day and all night. Also, there is no one to direct the robots, so they keep on packing nothing."

"It makes sense," said Jeremy thoughtfully.

"But one day they'll start to wear out, and then they'll have to stop," added Charlotte.

"In that case," Jeremy said, "there must be a place nearby where those people used to live. We should try to find it and discover what happened to them."

They both knew that trouble was ahead, but neither dared say it.

The children stepped into the courtyard which surrounded the factory, trying to dodge the boxes which kept tumbling down. They soon found a narrow road which wound in and out of the factory buildings.

"Let's go this way," suggested Charlotte, pointing where the pathway seemed to be less bothered by the falling boxes.

All three walked beside the factory wall, one behind the other. Through the many windows they could see that in every factory building were more of the machines. The wheels were spinning, the platforms were high with boxes and the silvery robots rushed about in mad activity.

The pathway continued on and on until it turned a corner into a wide square. Yet another curious sight lay before the travellers. Once again the ground was strewn with hundreds of boxes which were falling from the huge piles. But here they were being gathered up by large, busy, cleaning machines. These machines were tearing the boxes into small pieces, which were then put into sacks. Other machines carried the sacks of torn-up boxes over to the giant spinning wheels and emptied them somewhere into the top. Then they went back for more.

"It's really quite crazy," said Charlotte. "The pieces are being turned back into boxes by the spinning wheels. Then they go down the belt to the packing robots. The robots pack them too high, so they fall off, into the yard. Then the cleaning machines gather them, tear them up, and put them back into the spinning wheels – to be turned back into boxes again! It can go on forever. They are making the same boxes out of the same material. Yes, it's really crazy!"

"Alright, alright," said Jeremy quickly. He didn't want Charlotte to continue any more, in case *she* went on forever. "I agree, but we'll find the answer to this soon."

He was about to say something else when he stopped, with a hoot of excitement. He had spotted a small car standing beside one of the doorways. It was shaped something like a pram, and was resting on thin, shiny, yellow rails. The children crowded close and looked inside. There was a narrow seat, and the only controls appeared to be two buttons, one red and the other green.

"Obviously START and STOP," said Jeremy importantly. He clambered inside, sitting down on the seat which was only big enough for two.

"Twitch will have to sit on my lap," called Charlotte. As she sat down Twitch hastily jumped in after her. "It must be automatic," Charlotte continued, "and those two buttons control it. See how the rails twist and twine through the factory buildings? We must try it."

Without further delay, she pressed the green button. Immediately the little car started to trundle forward, into and round about the factories at first, but soon turning away towards the open country.

It was very pleasant riding along like that. The grass and trees looked fresh and green. The sun was warm, but the little breeze caused by the movement of the car kept them cool. Therefore it seemed all too soon that they found they were nearing some white buildings which they hadn't been able to see from the factory windows. As they drew closer, they saw how delicately the buildings were made, with fragile, slender spires that rang like wine glasses as the breeze stroked them. Once again the feeling of empty silence came upon the children.

The car was slowing down because the rails were coming to an end. It stopped and the three passengers stepped down. At once the car started off again, returning in the direction of the factories, and was soon lost to sight.

"Well," said Charlotte, a little bit concerned, "we cannot go back that way, even if we wanted to." Her concern did not last long, and she turned round, excitedly, to examine the little village in which they now found themselves.

The children's first impression was of emptiness. They had half hoped there would be someone there, when they had seen it in the distance. The streets were deserted and lifeless. Not even an animal or a bird moved or sang.

"We'll have to look in the houses," decided Jeremy.

Without comment Charlotte followed him up the steps and onto the porch of the nearest house. Just a little way along there was an open window, and with some nervousness the children peered through. They had an enormous surprise. Lying on a couch were three children, fast asleep. Two of them were girls, with long, fair hair, and the third was a boy whose hair was almost black. They did not stir in their sleep, and lay so still that they hardly appeared to be breathing. They were all dressed alike, in silver trousers and jackets, and had big, brightly coloured badges on their sleeves.

Quietly, Jeremy and Charlotte tip-toed back down the steps, and started to look through the windows of the other houses. Soon they found that everywhere was the same. The village was full of children, and all of them in a deep sleep.

"Do you realise," Jeremy said, "these are the missing people. The ones who must run the factories. No wonder everything seems to be going wrong there. They can't look after the robots and the machines if they're asleep. They must be the Machine Children."

Charlotte nodded. Jeremy was almost certainly right – but what terrible disaster had affected the Machine Children, and sent them so deeply asleep that the factories had fallen into a state of utter madness?

"We must go right in," declared Charlotte. "Look, most of the doors are open already. We must try to wake one of them."

With Charlotte leading the way, the children climbed the steps again, towards one of the doors which was swinging wide open. Feeling rather as though they were trespassing, they stepped through and entered the house. For a moment they stood looking down at the two sleeping boys they found inside. Then Charlotte bent over and gently shook the nearest boy's shoulder.

Not a movement, nor a flicker of his eyelids resulted. It was as if she had not even touched him. She reached down again, shaking harder – then even harder still, but there was no response of any kind.

"Its no use," she said slowly. "He just cannot be woken. Whatever has made all these children fall asleep? It certainly isn't natural."

As she spoke she started to rub her hands together, for they felt uncomfortable and dry. When she looked closely, she saw they were covered with a fine, grey dust. "Where did that come from?" she wondered to herself, and she knelt, so as to look more closely at the sleeping figures. They were both thickly covered by the same grey dust, and Charlotte could now see that it covered everything: the bed, the furniture, the floor and the walls.

"For all this dust to have gathered," she said to Jeremy, "they must have been asleep for years!" She felt her nose tickling and itching, and in a second she was sneezing and sneezing as if she would never stop.

It must have been this sneezing fit that saved them all. Without it, this story would end right here, because by the time it was over, and Charlotte turned round, she saw, to her great horror that both Jeremy and Twitch had joined the sleeping boys, and were fast asleep on the floor.

Charlotte felt her own eyes growing heavy, and her whole body became weak with a great tiredness. She yawned several times, and was almost ready to lay down when alarm bells seemed to ring in her brain.

"It must be the dust!" she exclaimed. "It is deadly! It has sent everyone in the village to sleep, even Jeremy and Twitch. Now it's beginning to get to me."

Realising that she had to keep herself awake, she dashed out into the street, where the air was a little fresher. Even here there were traces of the dust, and that was why it was so still and quiet. Even the birds and animals were probably asleep. Taking her handkerchief, she tied it over her mouth and nose to keep the dust out, then she sat down on the steps to think.

"What is there I can do to get rid of it?" she wondered. "The dust is all around, covering everything so thickly."

Despite her mask, Charlotte began to feel more and more drowsy, and her mind was nearly refusing to think, when she remembered the green-stone ring. Through a haze of sleepiness she took the ring from her finger, and breathed gently onto it. The last thing she remembered, before her eyes closed, was that the ring grew warm, then hot, then so hot that she could no longer hold it, and then, as the ring fell to the ground, her head nodded forward and in no time at all she was fast asleep.

The ring dropped noiselessly onto the ground and for a second or two lay there. Would it really be able to help the children, as the deemy had promised? Certainly something was now happening, for a thin streak of fire began to glow, deep within the green stone. The fire grew brighter and then, suddenly, a terrible flash of lightning hurtled from it, up into the sky. From nowhere, great black clouds started to gather, the sun was covered and the sky became dark and cold. There was another scorching flash from the stone, and in the following silence, rain started to fall.

At first there were just a few drops, scattered here and there, making round dents on the dusty ground, but rapidly the drops became bigger and came down faster. Very soon, the rain was falling in an absolute flood, covering the ground in a sheet of water, which grew deeper and deeper until it was a foot, or more, deep, lapping over the first of the steps on which Charlotte lay. Deafening claps of thunder shook and echoed around the village, making the slender roofs and spires split and shatter, and the rain flooded down through the broken roofs, washing everything it touched. Such was its force that soon every trace of the dust had been swept away.

As the last of the sleeping-dust was cleansed from the village, all the children started to awake. First one, then another sat up, eyes wide open. They yawned and stretched their arms and legs, after their long sleep, and they looked around in surprise at the broken roofs and spires. They talked to each other excitedly as they pointed to the great pools of water now fast draining away into the ground.

Charlotte had been quickly woken as the rain fell upon her, and she called out anxiously, "Jeremy! Twitch! Where are you? Are you alright?"

Immediately, Jeremy and Twitch came running to her. It was strange – neither of them could remember falling asleep. They looked around at the damage, and saw the village children, all wide awake, and then Charlotte told them what she had done. By the time she had finished, the rain had stopped, and a friendly sun was once again shining.

As Jeremy and Charlotte stood there, on the steps, the Machine Children gathered around, drifting from the little houses until a silent, smiling crowd surrounded them. One of the boys stepped forward – he was taller than the rest, and looked older, and must have been a leader, for his clothes were of gold instead of the usual silver. He held both hands out towards Jeremy and Charlotte, and then he spoke.

"Thank you for waking us," he said quietly. "The dust must have come down on us silently, and without warning, many years ago. None of us know for certain, but we believe that it was sent by the Spiderking, who collected it thousands of years in the past, when the two dark stars of death collided, and shattered into dust. The Spiderking is at war with us. He hates everything that brings happiness, and he intends to destroy us all."

Jeremy and Charlotte looked at each other uneasily. This Spiderking sounded really terrible.

"He must be very angry at what we have done, cleaning away the dust," Charlotte said.

Then the leader of the Machine Children spoke again: "Although we have been saved this time, the Spiderking will try again and again and will never rest until he manages to destroy us, or he is destroyed."

Charlotte had been thinking. Her head was tilted to one side, and there was a frown on her face. "Why does the creature hate you so much?" she asked. "You seem to be so very quiet and peaceful."

The leader of the Machine Children spoke sadly: "We spend our lives growing crystals of peace on our trees of helpfulness." He pointed to where a number of trees were growing – trees with reddish-brown branches and leaves.

"It must have been one of those that helped us over the wall," whispered Jeremy, and Charlotte nodded.

The boy continued, "When the crystals are ready we take them to the factories, where they are carefully packed by silver robots." Charlotte and Jeremy looked at each other, and smiled. "Then they are sent to every part of the universe. Every planet, and every sun. Every comet and every star. They bring peace and contentment, and they help in the fight against evil and wickedness. Now that we are awake, we must get the factories going again."

Charlotte could hardly wait for the boy to stop talking. Eagerly, she told him how they had seen the factories and the silver robots.

"Everything is still working fine," she said, "except that the boxes are now all empty."

The leader of the Machine-Children smiled as he replied, "Our task seems as though it will be easier than I thought. I wondered if the Spiderking had destroyed the factories, but I suppose he did not bother as he thought that we would never be awake again to work in them."

He looked solemnly at the children and said, "It's our great good fortune that you are here," he said. "But why did you come? We have few visitors to this land."

Speaking together, Jeremy and Charlotte told of their adventures in seeking the seven keys, and how they now expected that they would find the next one somewhere on this world. As they spoke, the faces of the Machine Children grew worried and serious.

"You have made a terrible enemy in the Spiderking," the leader said. "Your search is therefore going to be even more dangerous. To find the next key you must go to his castle. There is a story that we have known ever since we were born. A story that tells of a magic key, hidden deep in the Spiderking's maze. Many have tried to find it, they have entered the maze and have wandered for days, hopelessly lost, and none have ever returned. It is said that the Spiderking watches their every movement, and laughs as he enjoys their misery and despair, until they finally sink to the ground, starving and exhausted, never to rise again. Now the Spiderking knows that you have helped us, he will make everything you do much more difficult. I'm very sorry."

"Oh don't be so upset," Charlotte said. "We can only win the keys by helping others. So, by helping you our pathway to the keys must be a little clearer. We won't be afraid of the Spiderking, and you'll see that, one day, we'll return safely."

As she finished speaking, Jeremy said, "Sh! Listen." From the only delicate spire that remained unharmed by the storm, a beautiful chiming noise began to sound in the quiet air. Soft at first, it grew louder and then still louder until the sound seemed to come from every stone, echoing back from the walls of the houses around. When every face was turned towards the spire, the musical sound stopped, and a small door of the spire swung open, wide.

The leader of the children turned towards the small stairway that led up to the door. As if in a dream, he walked to the foot of the stairway, and half-way there he stopped and turned.

"Charlotte! Jeremy!" he softly called. "You must come with me. Here, take my hands," and he held his arms out towards the two children.

Together, they climbed the stairs and came to the open door. As they stopped in front of it, Jeremy whispered to Charlotte, "I didn't see this building before, did you?" Charlotte shook her head.

Then the leader of the Machine Children spoke again: "Now you must go in by yourselves," he said. "What you'll find is for your eyes only."

Jeremy and Charlotte heard him quietly turn and return down the stairs to join the other children. With a feeling of excitement Jeremy and Charlotte stepped into the cool, dim room. The chiming noise started again, but softer now and sounding as though a long way away. They took two more steps forward, and then both cried out in surprise. In an instant, there appeared in front of them, floating in the air, a whirling, twirling, many-coloured ball of light. As it

116

twisted and turned, it touched first Jeremy, then Charlotte, sparkling and flashing with each contact. When this happened, they each felt a warm glow of gladness and hope that, somehow was mixed with memories of the Fountain of Happiness, and the days when their mother and father were still with them.

The children felt unable to move, fixed to the spot by the thoughts and memories brought to their minds by the magic light. They stayed like that for a few moments.

Quite suddenly, the ball of light began to grow smaller and smaller. As it did so, it grew so bright that they could hardly bear to look at it. At that very moment, with a last brilliant flash, it ceased to float in the air and dropped onto Jeremy's hand – and then it was gone.

Jeremy was so surprised he could hardly think. He stared at his hand. For a moment, after such brightness, the darkness inside the room stopped him from seeing anything at all. Then he realised that there was something hard within the palm of his hand. Slowly he opened his fingers, and with eyes now grown used to the dim light, both children found that they were looking at a small, almost completely square, glass key.

"The next key!" Charlotte exclaimed.

They walked out from the small room and down the stairway. The Machine Children were still gathered around. Their leader walked forward, and he was smiling happily.

"Before you leave," he said, "we have something for you. Wear these round your necks, and never take them off. They are crystals of Peace, and will help you whenever you feel unhappy, tired or miserable – and if you are ever in real need, they will, just once, come to your help."

Jeremy and Charlotte gazed at the beautiful, glowing crystals, and Twitch stood up on his back legs to see more clearly. As the crystals hung around the children's necks they glowed softly in the bright sunshine. Then they turned and looked away, towards the far distance, and they knew that it was time to go.

"Which way must we take, to the castle of the Spiderking?" asked Jeremy quietly, and the leader stood beside him and pointed.

"Do you see that dull, red star?" he asked. "It hangs low over the

Spiderking's home. It's a star of dread and evil. Make your way towards it, and you will find the Spiderking. There you will find the maze – and the seventh key. All our hearts are sad to see you leave, but our wishes for success will be with you every moment."

With a final wave, Jeremy, Charlotte and Twitch set off on the final part of their journey. Their thoughts were heavy with dread as they trudged onwards. The village of the Machine Children faded away into the distance behind them.

SPIDER MAZE

The dusty, stony grass stretched on and on, behind the children, on both sides, and far into the distance ahead. All day long they trudged, at first talking with great excitement about the factories, the machines and the Machine Children, and the sleep-dust. They grew silent as the hours passed and the heat of the day seeped into every bone of their bodies. By late afternoon, the village of the Machine Children was just a memory, miles away, and it might only have been a half-remembered dream but for the sixth key, safely tucked away to prove that it had all really happened.

Now and again one of the children would think of something that made them both smile. On one occasion Jeremy said with a laugh, "Fancy all those robots rushing around so filled with importance – filling hundreds of boxes with nothing."

Charlotte laughed also as she replied, "They seemed so eager to keep on working. Never mind. At least, now that the children are all awake again the crystals will soon be ready for packing."

As she spoke, Charlotte glanced upwards and was surprised to see that the clouds overhead were becoming thicker and darker. The evening was growing late, and now the red star seemed to fill the gloomy sky, glaring like the eye of a devil, low on the horizon.

"I'm tired," Charlotte said. "My legs ache."

"I'm tired too," Jeremy said.

"We must stop and rest."

Jeremy nodded, without speaking, and Twitch sat down with a small "Meow" of agreement. Taking her cloak, Charlotte spread it on the ground, and sat down with a tired sigh. Jeremy joined her and Twitch snuggled down close to him.

Charlotte took a small box from her pocket.

"Where did you get that?" Jeremy asked. "What is it? I've never seen that before."

Charlotte smiled, and then she told him that, just before they had left the village, the Machine Children had given it to her, to help them on their way. As she opened the box, both children gave gasps of delight. Packed tightly inside were tasty looking cakes.

"This is great!" Jeremy mumbled, his mouth already full. "It's nice to have a sweet once in a while."

For a while there was silence as they ate, hardly able to take their eyes from the glaring red star. Under its dim light they fancied that they could see the walls of a great castle. That must be their target, looming far away in the distance, but their minds were troubled as they finally fell asleep. They had also noticed strange moving lights that lay in between them and the home of the Spiderking.

Neither slept well that night for their dreams were a mixture of excitement and dread. Excited as they were at being so close to that last key, they were chilled at what they had been told of the terrible and evil Spiderking.

Awakening at the first light of dawn they were soon on their way again, watching the last pale stars fade as the sun showed above the horizon. In the bright light of day, the red star seemed less frightening. Besides, in the bright sunlight the children could see the faint outlines of a great castle – black against the blue of the sky. They had been travelling along a rough road of grass and stones, but all at once this came to an end. Instead, under their feet was a red, dusty path. But it was only a mile or two before this also ended, and stretching out in front of the children was nothing but desert.

The grass and bushes had all disappeared, leaving only a featureless, baking hot expanse of sand. The sun's rays reflected in great blinding waves of burning heat from a sky that was a shimmering bowl of fire. Harsh cries of huge birds filled the children's ears.

Looking upwards, Jeremy said, "What birds are those?"

"I don't know," Charlotte replied, "but they appear to be harmless."

None came down towards the children, although, many times they swooped low to snatch small creatures from the ground.

The fierceness of the sun's rays grew worse with every minute, parching the children's throats, and burning their arms and legs. The brilliant light, reflecting from the shining sands hurt their eyes and made it difficult for them to see where they were going.

The red star was always there, and so the children knew that they could not lose their way, whatever the difficulties.

"Poor old Twitch," said Charlotte at one point. "How on earth can you stand this heat, with all that hot fur?"

Twitch was, indeed, so hot and bothered that he could not find the strength to answer.

The light from the sun now seemed to be of a greenish colour, and although it blazed down all that morning, burning their skin, the air began to feel strangely cold.

Sometime in the early afternoon Jeremy first noticed the little puffs of sand that were lifting into the air. At first they did not seem important, but when they continued, and grew more numerous, Jeremy pointed them out to Charlotte. As she looked where he was pointing she frowned.

"That's strange," she said with. "There's no wind, not even a breeze to cause them."

As the children stopped to watch, several more of the sand-puffs lifted, and then collapsed slowly. From the corner of her eye Charlotte thought she saw some of them take on strange and forbidding shapes. Quickly she turned her head to look at them, but as soon as she did so, they were gone. With great unease the children saw that the shapes were now getting closer and more numerous.

"Do you see those things?" Charlotte asked Jeremy in a shaky voice. "I'm sure they're beginning to look like some kind of three legged imp."

Jeremy did not have time to answer. There was a terrible clap of thunder, and in a blast of fiery, hot wind, a dense cloud of dust rose into the air, getting into the children's mouths, and filling their eyes so that they had to screw them up tight. Charlotte reached out for Jeremy and Twitch, and held them close.

Slowly the dust swirled and settled. The air cleared, leaving the children's mouths dry, Their eyes smarted as they fearfully looked around, and then both cried out in terror, for they found that they were surrounded by a band of ugly, evil-looking, black imps.

The children studied the imps with amazement. Their first impression was blackness, total, absolute blackness from head to toe, with eyes of smoking green that glared through narrow slits out of a scaly skin. Each imp had three squat legs and thin, twisting tails that were forever moving, wriggling and twisting like long, black snakes. The imps stood still, their eyes fixed on the children, and now and again, one of them would make a threatening movement with the sharp, black fork that he carried in his clawed, bony fingers.

After several minutes, the imp who appeared to be in charge spoke in a hard, hissing voice, placing his face within inches of the children's – so close that they could smell the sharp, vinegary smell of the creature's skin.

"What are you doing here?" it demanded. "You have invaded the private land of the Spiderking, and you will suffer for doing so. Come now, answer quickly or we'll have fun killing you with our devil-forks."

As he said this, the children's horrified eyes saw the forks squirm in the imp's hands, and they could see that every fork had thin, red eyes that glared at them over a cruel slit of a mouth. A forked black tongue flickered in and out of the mouth and, like a snake, the tongue dripped with poison.

Charlotte spoke quickly, "We're looking for the seven keys."

The imps cackled with laughter, making Charlotte so angry that she forgot to be frightened any more.

"Well," said the imp leader, "you have, for sure, now reached the end of your travels. We'll stop all that nonsense. We'll take you to our master, the Spiderking, and he'll make you amuse him – if you are lucky. Otherwise, he'll eat you straight away."

Surrounded by the imps, and constantly menaced by the devil-forks, the children set off again, onwards towards the castle, and for the rest of the day they travelled across the burning dust, with no rest, and no food or drink.

Poor Twitch, on his little feet, was exhausted, and Charlotte had to carry him in case he lagged behind, and gave the imps the excuse to try out their devil-forks on him.

All that day they marched, forever onwards until the black walls of the castle could be plainly seen. The children were so tired that they could hardly lift their feet from the dry sand. At long last, the blazing sun sank, giving way to the cool of the evening.

The children saw that they were so close to the castle that the red star was almost overhead. Its evil, red light lit everything with a sickly glow, reflecting oddly from the scales on the imps and shining horribly from the eyes of their forks.

The castle was now directly in front of the children. It was immense, with wide, dark walls – but built low on the ground, monstrous and squat.

"Only a foul creature such as the Spiderking could live in such a place," Charlotte whispered.

The red light of the star reflected from the windows like blood, and in its miserable glow the imps took on an appearance even more frightening than before. They danced and jumped around Jeremy and Charlotte, pretending to stab with their forks, all the time pushing the children nearer and nearer to the castle walls.

Suddenly all the movement and dancing stopped. The imps fell back behind the children in a long, unmoving line. Their leader spoke: "Go!" he said, pointing his devil fork.

As the children moved forward, the red tongues on the forks flickered wildly, and the eyes flashed in anger at seeing the children leave, unharmed.

Jeremy and Charlotte walked towards the great castle door in front of them. Charlotte glanced back over her shoulder and said, "The imps have disappeared."

"Let's run away," Jeremy said.

"No," Charlotte replied. "We must beat the Spiderking to win the last key."

They walked silently for a few minutes, then Charlotte said, "Don't worry. It's only a spider, after all."

"I hate spiders," Jeremy grumbled, "I hope it's a small one."

It seemed an age, but those final steps to the castle could only have taken a minute or two. At last the children were standing at the low, wide door they had seen from far away. The surface of the door was flat. There was no bell, no knocker, and no handle of any kind. The wood was old and twisted, and seemed to have within it the outlines of devilish faces, with faint shapes of eyes that followed their every movement. Ignoring these strange figures Charlotte lifted her hand and hammered on the door with her fist, and the noise echoed from every stone in the castle walls.

There was a rapid scuffling noise from the other side. Just as the children thought that the door was about to open, a slithering, crackling noise over their heads made them look up. They barely had time to see a cloud of something falling upon them. The next moment they were entangled in a mass of thin, steel-like sticks, and a silken mesh. They found themselves being drawn slowly upwards, swaying, struggling and kicking, but making no impression on whatever it was that held them.

Up and up they rose, alongside the castle wall, and then, with a jerk, they came to a stop. For a moment or two they hung there, twisting and twirling around, first this way, then back again until they began to feel quite dizzy. By now the moon was clear in the sky, and by its pale light Charlotte could see the silken threads that held them firmly.

"It's a giant spider's web!" she exclaimed.

Almost before she had finished saying it the web started to move again. They were lifted high over the castle turrets. It was only a short journey this time. With a bump, they were dropped in a heap onto a cold, moss-covered stone floor.

"Are you alright?" Charlotte whispered.

"I've bumped my head," Jeremy said.

"Meow," said a frightened Twitch.

"What's this humming noise?" Jeremy said. "Is it in my head?"

"No, I can hear it too," Charlotte said.

"And the smell!" Jeremy said, twisting his nose.

"It's the same smell as the imps," Charlotte said.

Brilliant, yellow light streamed through an open door across the courtyard. There was a grinding, shuffling noise from within.

"Enter!" roared a harsh, grating voice.

Although they had no wish to obey, their feet began to move, urged on by some unknown force. Crossing the floor, they stepped through the doorway.

For a moment or two they could see nothing. The light was so bright after the dim redness outside that their eyes took a while to get used to it – and then they almost wished they hadn't. The sight in front of them was the most dreadful they could ever have imagined, and they shrank back in horror, almost crying out in overwhelming fear.

In the centre of a huge, round room was an enormous platform, upon which squatted a colossal black spider. Its eyes were like green fire and its mouth was a yellow slit which hardly moved as it spoke.

"Come right in!" it ordered.

Thick, black webs hung draping down from above, almost touching the children's heads. Over the webs crawled thousands of ugly spiders, dropping to the floor and climbing up again, moving in dozens in and out, and around the platform on which the giant spider rested. From every part of the room their evil eyes stared.

"I have known, for a long time, that you were coming," the Spiderking said. "How dare you trespass in MY kingdom, interfering with MY plans and plotting to steal MY magic key? It is MINE! Do you hear? MINE only!"

The Spiderking's eyes rolled in rage as it thumped up and down on the platform, sending a hoard of the black spiders scurrying across the floor.

"You will suffer for this," it continued. "You'll suffer even more for the way you meddled with my plans for the Machine Children." At this point the Spiderking became so enraged that its mouth frothed horribly and started to twist in every direction at once.

"It's not very pleased with us," Jeremy whispered. He then laughed as he saw that Twitch was sitting there with both paws over his eyes.

Charlotte nodded. "We must find the key," she whispered to Jeremy. "We'll find a way to destroy the Spiderking."

The giant spider rose to its feet and thundered its sixteen legs up and down onto the platform, over and over, squashing and destroying many of the other spiders as it did so. The whole room shook, sending showers of the revolting black spiders down from the roof and onto the children. Charlotte screamed as they tangled in her hair, but Jeremy, quick as a flash, brushed them away, stamping on them with both feet.

The sight of the enraged Spiderking was quite incredible, and should have been dreadfully frightening. But by now the children had completely regained their courage, and they were nowhere near as scared as they had been earlier. Even Twitch had, more or less recovered.

The huge spider stretched forward, and its head was so close that the children stepped back hastily from its horrible hot breath.

"I hate the Machine Children most of all," it growled. "So I sent the dust of eternal sleep, and as it settled over their village, I knew that I had won. There would be no more crystals, and the machines would only be making empty boxes, while the stupid robots would be filling them with nothing! And so it would go on forever. There would be no more peace and everyone would hate one another. I decided that, when I felt like it, I would send the imps and set them loose in the village with their forks."

In a tremendous roar of rage the Spiderking screamed at the children, "But you – you wretched two-legged creatures – you have ruined my plans!"

The children stood frozen to the spot at the sight of this giant spider, screaming, shouting, thumping and banging in uncontrollable temper.

Charlotte was unable to keep quiet, she was so filled with disgust and anger at what the spider had said. In a loud, furious voice she shouted back at the monster, "You were evil and wicked to send the dust – the Machine Children were doing you no harm. Whatever happens, we are glad we managed to stop your selfish plans from working. You'll not be able to do it again. We know that you can't get any more of the sleep dust."

The Spiderking had never been spoken to like that before. It turned purple with fury, swelling up until Charlotte really thought that there was a chance that it might burst. In a voice so filled with hate that the children would hardly understand what it was saying, it spluttered an order to its unseen guards: "Take them away! Remove them from my sight before I seize them and tear them apart. Destroying them quickly would be too kind after what they have done to my plans. Instead, they shall be thrown into the maze."

The Spiderking rolled its eyes and laughed deep in its throat before continuing, "Yes, throw them into the maze. I shall watch every movement as they wander around and around for days – maybe weeks, hopelessly lost, until they die. Their bones will join those of the hundreds of others who have dared to anger me."

Again the horrible laughter escaped from the monster's twisted mouth, and the hot, vinegary breath puffed out across the children making them sick with disgust. But, before they had time to think of what might be about to happen, the web fell upon them again. Struggling fiercely, they were dragged along a foul-smelling hallway towards a small, wooden door.

Fortunately for them, the door was not far away, for the ground was hard and rocky and there was no way that they could protect their arms and legs from being banged and scratched as they were tumbled over and over in the web. It was only a minute or two before they reached the door.

The next second found themselves thrown headlong through it and onto the stony ground outside the castle walls.

"Not a very nice spider," said Twitch in an annoyed voice, dusting himself down, and shaking the fluff from his whiskers. "But at least we are out of the castle."

Having finished tidying himself up he then sat up and curled his tail around his paws. For some odd reason he started to purr noisily.

Charlotte was still sitting where she had landed, staring into space and making no attempt to brush the mud from her clothes. "Oh, shut up!" she suddenly said.

Twitch stared at her in amazement. Turning his back on her, he started to sulk.

"Oh dear," thought Jeremy, "Now he'll be like that all day!"

Charlotte turned towards Jeremy and said, "Did you hear what the Spiderking said?"

"Yes," said Jeremy.

"Well, we must be exactly where he said we'd be thrown: in the maze. This must be where it starts."

Jeremy answered quietly, "Yes, and the creature told us we'll never find our way out."

"Never mind *what* he said," she snapped. "Of course we'll find our way through. But that's not all I was thinking about. Haven't you realised yet? Gosh, you must be dim today. *This* is the maze where the Seventh key is hidden."

Jeremy's mouth fell open in surprise. He had not even thought of this, he had been so frightened.

Even Twitch turned back to look at the children, and gave a happy little "Meow" as Charlotte stroked his head and said, "Sorry Twitch, let's be friends again."

They turned and looked about them. Behind them rose the castle walls and the wooden door, now firmly closed. In front and on both sides tall hedges reached up towards the sky, and between the hedges were a number of paths all leading in different directions. It was still night, and the only light was that from the dim red star which still hung low in the sky. The pathway looked dark and forbidding – filled with shadows and unseen dread.

"We'll rest," said Charlotte firmly, "We'll set off in the morning."

The others did not argue. They felt really worn out after their meeting with the Spiderking. They settled down to close their eyes and await the dawn.

Bright shafts of sunlight shining directly into their eyes awoke them. Charlotte and Jeremy got up eager to get going on their way, through the maze.

However, in the light of a new day they were able to see just how difficult their task was going to be. There were a number of paths, all leading in different direction. There were far more than they had been able to see in the dim red light of the previous evening.

Charlotte made no move, for several minutes, as she considered what they should do. "Wait," she said. "It's easy to wander in and out at random, and then find we've just been going round in circles."

"Let's form a plan," Jeremy suggested.

They sat for some minutes, but no ideas came into their mind.

Suddenly, Charlotte jumped up and said, "I know! We must be sure that we keep going onwards, and don't find ourselves coming back here."

"How?" Jeremy asked.

"See," Charlotte explained, "there's a faint moon still shining in the sky," and she pointed towards it. "Well, we'll use that to guide us, and if we follow its direction we won't get lost."

Without further waste of time they started off. Almost at once they found themselves deep within the maze, and soon nothing more could be seen of the red star or the black castle walls.

On and on they went, twisting one way, taking another, first forward, then to the side, then forward again. All the time they found more and more paths which tempted them this way, that way, any way. But the only road they took was that which led the most directly towards the moon which still shone in the blue sky above.

"I don't know what all the fuss was about," Jeremy said, "We have easily worked out what to do. We must be halfway through already."

It was just then that the troubles started. The pathway before them had been straight and wide for a while. Suddenly, it divided into several narrow tracks which led in every possible direction. Charlotte looked upwards to see where the moon was.

"It's gone!" she said.

"The sun is much too bright for moon," Jeremy added. "There's nothing to guide us now."

After a few moments of silence, Charlotte cheered up again and said, "It doesn't really matter. We were only using it to stop ourselves going round in circles. There was no way of knowing whether or not it was leading us towards the key."

"So what are we going to do?" Jeremy asked.

"I have another idea," Charlotte said. "When the road divides into several directions, we'll take the middle path. If it only divides into two, we'll go left first and then right the next time."

And that is exactly what they did. The path divided and twisted, turned and divided again. There were roadways to the side by the dozen, but at every difficult point they followed the rules thought up by Charlotte. They felt quite confident that by now they were successfully finding their way through the maze.

Forwards. Then a path to the left. Then one to the right – then forwards again. The hours passed by and the children became more and more hopeful with every step they took.

But, turning a corner they found the way blocked by a high, smooth wall. Their hearts sank as they heard the horrible laughter of the Spiderking.

"It must have been watching us!" Charlotte said angrily.

"How?" asked Jeremy.

"I don't know," Charlotte answered. "Let's go back. The wall's too high to climb."

Trudging unhappily along, they walked back down the path for a long, long distance until they came to one of the side turnings that they had passed earlier in the day. They turned off, glad that they were now on new ground again.

But it did not take long for them to realise that they were now in real trouble.

"Look, Charlotte," Jeremy said, pointing at a red stone, "this is the same stone we saw when we first started – we've been walking all day and have got nowhere . . ."

Then the ugly, mocking laughter rang out, echoing again and again until they put their hands over their ears to try to shut it out.

Charlotte jumped to her feet. This time the laughter had an amazing effect, and she was boiling with rage.

"Come on, you two," she ordered, "that stupid, ridiculous monster will *never* beat us! We've already proven that we can win. We've destroyed its sleep-dust, and now we'll show that this maze is a lot of nonsense!"

In the distance, the cackling laughter was replaced by a growl of anger, and the children felt pleased as they realised that their remarks had been heard, and had spoiled the Spiderking's pleasure.

So they set off again with fresh determination taking, as before, first a turn to the left and than a turn to the right – until Jeremy came to a sudden stop.

Indeed, it was so sudden that Twitch, who never looked where he was going, walked right into Jeremy's legs, bumping his nose with a loud "Meow!" Sitting upright, the cat complained in annoyance.

"Hey, be more careful. Why did" . . . . He stopped because he saw what had made Jeremy halt so suddenly. There was a shadowy corner where the hedges met and from it came a pale gleam of white. All three travellers looked in horrified silence at the small heap of bones which lay on the ground – one of the victims of the maze, no doubt, who had never found the way out.

Without a word, the children turned away, and Twitch became very quiet, walking nervously between them. No one felt like talking as they pressed onwards. First left, then right. Right, then left. They walked for hours.

It was Jeremy who, rounding a bend, stopped again. In front of him was a very familiar red stone. The children saw, with shocked dismay that, once again, they were back where they had started.

"It's hopeless," said Jeremy, sinking to the ground with his face in his hands. "We can never find our way out now. We'll go round and round until we end up as heaps of bones like the ones we saw earlier."

At his words the harsh, crashing laughter thundered out yet again and Charlotte pressed her hands over her ears to shut out the sound. As she did so, her hand brushed against the Crystal which hung around her neck. She remembered the words of the Machine Children. "It would help, just once," they had told her. Now she would test it. How it might lead them from the maze, she had no idea.

With fresh strength and hope she sprang to her feet. She raised the crystal high above her head. Jeremy was now standing beside her, and the children saw that, as the afternoon rays of the sun shone upon it, the crystal began to turn slowly, first one way and then the other. Odd colours and shapes gleamed within it, but although it continued to swing to and fro, nothing more seemed to happen.

Jeremy turned disappointed eyes towards Charlotte, and was about to speak when she put her fingers to her lips, to warn him to stay silent. Puzzled, he turned back towards the crystal, and then he became aware that something was beginning to happen. All noise around them was gradually fading away until there was utter, complete silence.

Charlotte stepped to the side, turning her head to face Jeremy – and at once the sounds all around started again. She turned back to where she had stood before. Once more, silence! There was no sound to be heard – not her feet on the ground, nor the wind blowing in the trees high overhead, not even the cackle of the Spiderking. Nothing. Several times she turned, testing the different directions, and she found that on every side except one, she could hear everything – but in that one direction – silence!

Jeremy had been watching her step backwards, forwards, to one side, then another in growing surprise. "What are you doing?"

Charlotte explained about the sound and silence.

"Well", said Jeremy, "surely it's trying to tell us which is the right direction to take."

"Of course!" Charlotte exclaimed. "You've got it Jeremy! Look, as we turn around there is only one direction where the sound stops. Every other direction is normal, and we can hear all the usual noises. We must follow the silence. That's the answer."

So, in single file, step by step and with regained happiness they walked onwards, and whenever they turned in the wrong direction they were warned at once, for all the noises that filled the air could be heard again. There was one particular noise they could not hear and it would have filled them with amusement if they had. It was the humming, growling fury of the Spiderking who now realised that they were escaping from his trap.

For a long time they followed the guide of silence, never daring to stop to eat, drink or rest, for fear that the magic of the crystal might be lost. At one point Jeremy asked Charlotte if she really thought that they were going the right way, and she replied with a smile, "I hope so – and I really do think that we are. Haven't you noticed that we have not been stopped by any walls today?"

"There's only one thing that worries me," she confessed. "What happens when we stop and go to sleep? Will the crystal switch off and on again tomorrow?"

"Maybe we should stay awake," Jeremy replied.

"We can't," Charlotte said. "We must go to sleep sometime. I'm exhausted." As she spoke she yawned and so did Jeremy.

Charlotte dropped the haversack to the ground and sat down. Jeremy stretched out on his cloak and was asleep instantly.

As she closed her eyes, Charlotte thought of the last key. "We'll get it tomorrow," she thought. Soon she was as sound asleep as the others.

Charlotte was the first awake, just as the sun was beginning to rise. She leaned over, and shook Jeremy's arm. But, as she did so, she realised, with a sinking feeling that once more she could hear the wind, and the pattering of rain which was now falling fast. In a sudden panic she put her hand to her throat. Had the crystal used up all its magic and melted away, as she had feared?

"It's still here," she said with relief. The crystal still hung safely round her neck, and as she turned to her side silence fell again.

Without losing any more time, the children gathered their cloaks and the haversack and set off down the narrow, wet path.

They saw many more piles of bones along their pathway. So many others had found their way through the maze, even as far as this, and still fallen victim to the Spiderking's evil, in the end.

Charlotte had scarcely been looking around her, or thinking where she was going, when she was startled by Twitch. The cat had been walking ahead and was now dashing back, full of excitement.

"What is it, Twitch?" asked Jeremy. "What's the matter with you?" But before there was time for an answer, the children rounded a last bend. Then they could see for themselves. In the centre of the path was a gigantic stone, so immense that until they came really close to it they could not see past. Then, squeezing by, they found themselves in a wide clearing, with hundreds of paths leading into it – and every path was blocked by a similar stone.

"This must be the absolute centre of the maze", whispered Charlotte, and Jeremy nodded, eyes round and mouth open in wonder. There, in the middle of the clearing was a small, shining pond. Slowly the children walked towards it.

When they drew very close they saw a number of fish swimming backwards and forwards beneath the silvery waters. The fish were of different sizes and colours. Some were red, some blue, some were gold, and there was just one which had gleaming silver scales. As the children watched them in fascination, Charlotte felt the crystal begin to hum and vibrate as it hung round her neck. Then, to her wonder, the humming noise seemed to form words. Although these were no more than a whisper, both children could hear the words clearly.

"The key is here, guarded by one of the fish. You must choose the right one, but each of you has only one chance. If you fail, the key will be lost forever, and the Spiderking will claim you for his own."

Charlotte looked at the fish. Jeremy, Twitch and herself would each be able to choose, just the once. That made three chances only – but she could see at a glance that there were far more fish to choose from than the three chances they would have!

"It'll be impossible," she cried. "How can we choose the right one from so many, when we only have the one chance each?"

The voice did not answer, and the crystal became still and quiet. For a while, the children stood wondering what to do.

Twitch stared at the fish longingly, watching them sparkling and swimming backwards and forwards – all within a paw's reach. Suddenly, it all became too much for him. In a flash, and before either Jeremy or Charlotte could stop him, his paw darted out and he scooped one of the blue fish from the water. With a wide cat-like smile of delight, he bit it in half and in two seconds had swallowed it with a look of enormous enjoyment.

Jeremy and Charlotte looked at him in dismay. While they were wondering what would now happen, they heard the soft chime of a bell and a quiet, deep voice spoke. "The furry creature has chosen wrongly, his chance has gone."

The children looked at one another hopelessly, and then at the cat. Twitch suddenly realised what he had done and, in shamed distress crept over to a corner, and hid, with his paws over his eyes. All the children could see was his whiskers poking out.

The two thought for a while, and Jeremy said, "Listen, Charlotte, Twitch really hasn't done too badly after all. In a way he's really helped us, if you think about it." Jeremy turned around and called out to the cat. "Come over here, you silly old thing," he said.

Charlotte was still annoyed. "Twitch has lost us one of the only three chances we had to find the key. How can you say he has helped us?"

"Well," Jeremy replied said sharply, "just do as I say, and think about it. The red and blue fish are the same size, right?"

"I can see that without *you* telling me," she replied, still in an annoyed voice. "For goodness sake, get to the point!"

"I'm trying to." By now Jeremy was getting annoyed too, for

Charlotte did not seem to be making any attempt to understand him. "Just listen, will you? Twitch ate the blue fish in *only two bites.* If the fish was small enough for that, it would surely be too small to have the key inside!"

At that point Charlotte suddenly knew what Jeremy was saying, and she turned round with a jerk, her eyes shining.

"Oh, Jeremy," she said. "That's really clever. You are quite right. It cannot be the blue fish, and it can't be one of the red ones, for they are the same size."

Then Jeremy said thoughtfully, "That leaves one silver, one small golden fish, and one large golden fish. They are the only ones big enough. Three fish, but only two chances between us, so we can still lose, if we make one wrong choice. I'll choose one of the golden fish – you should take the silver."

Without waiting for Charlotte to reply, Jeremy looked down and said, "I choose you, little golden one."

The children waited in the silence that followed. Finally the bell chimed softly, but when the voice spoke, it sounded fainter, and sad.

"You have chosen wrongly," it said. "Your chance is gone, too."

Jeremy looked at Charlotte, and his eyes were full of fright. Both children knew that unless she chose correctly, they would never see the final key and they would never escape from the terrible world of the Spiderking. It was all up to her.

For a short time Charlotte watched the silver fish as it swam up and down, crossing from one side of the pool to the other. It was so bright, and its eyes gleamed like black buttons, outshining all the other fish in the water. They were strange, those eyes and they seemed to be looking deep into her mind and speaking to her – almost forcing her to speak. Still unable to take her eyes from the silver fish, she opened her mouth to call out the word "Silver."

Charlotte could never say what it was, afterwards, that set the alarm bells ringing in her mind. Perhaps the fish was *too* bright? Perhaps those button-like eyes were shining *too* much, but suddenly she felt that she was being *made* to choose the silver against her will! Without giving any more thought to what she was doing, she called out, "No! I do *not* want the silver one. I choose the second golden fish. You have the key!"

The pattering of the rain faded away and, within the pool the fishes stopped their endless swimming. The silver fish stopped, opposite to where the children stood and thrashed, and slapped its tail in a terrible rage. Its shining scales turned black, and its eyes turned to an angry red. With a snarling twist of its mouth, it faded away. As the children looked, all the other fish faded away too, except for one.

The golden fish remained. Under the fascinated eyes of the children it began to change. Its outlines blurred and it shimmered and glowed with a golden fire. It seemed to grow smaller, and it faded from their sight as the waters of the pond turned to breaths of mist which twisted and twirled thickly in the air above. Gradually the mist thinned, and floated away. Where the fish had been was now a solid block of gold.

Charlotte and Jeremy's stepped down onto the white stones which had once been the bottom of the pool. Reaching out, Charlotte touched the oddly shaped piece of gold, and as she did so she realised that the shape was that of a strange fish. She took hold of it and found it to be curiously heavy. As she examined it more closely, the outlines shifted, and blurred before her eyes, and it changed colours as it moved slightly in her hand.

Jeremy had watched closely as these odd things happened, and his face wore a puzzled frown as the two children stepped back onto the grass. For a moment they stood unmoving, looking at the object in Charlotte's hand.

It was then that it changed again. Firstly, as before, it blurred and shifted slightly. Then, in a cascade of brilliance, it changed colours a dozen times or more, flashing and sparkling and almost causing Charlotte to drop it. Then its blurred shape began to clear, and its golden colour faded. At last it was quiet and still, and both children also became quiet and still when they saw what was now resting in the palm of Charlotte's hand. A silvery – white stone, small and hard, yet warm to the touch, there lay the last, the seventh key.

"Now," breathed Charlotte, "we have them all."

Just that moment, when they all felt so glad, something light and immensely strong fell over their heads and shoulders.

Dread and despair suddenly replaced the feeling of joy in the children's minds. They knew at once that they had once more been captured in the web of the Spiderking. As they felt themselves being drawn upwards they shivered with fright at the thought of coming face to face with the horrible monster again. Twisting and swaying, high above the maze, they were speedily drawn back towards the castle. Spinning and turning, they struggled uselessly, held firmly within the web.

Then Charlotte remembered the crystal. Perhaps, in this last terrible moment it would help to set them free? Alas, as she reached for it she found it had gone, and she knew that its powers had been completely drained by its long search for the right path through the maze. A dreadful feeling of hopelessness filled her, and wave after wave of despair swept through her mind.

"What use will the seven keys be?" she thought, "if the Spiderking forever holds us prisoners?" She fell back against the side of the web, too weak to struggle further. As she leaned back against Jeremy, her eyes closed, she felt something scratch her face.

"Don't, Twitch", she murmured. "There's no way that you can cheer me up now!"

But, to her surprise, Twitch's answering "Meow" came from the other side of the web which held them captive.

"It can't be Twitch," Charlotte said to herself. "Then what is it that is digging into my face? It hurts!" She lay there for a moment or two, rubbing the place where her neck had been scratched. Then, in a flash of excitement, she remembered. Jeremy had been given one of the crystals, too. How silly to have forgotten!

"Jeremy!" she screamed loudly. She had to capture his attention quickly, they had so little time left. Already they were almost to the top of the castle walls and would soon be thrown back to the feet of the Spiderking.

"Jeremy!" she screamed, louder still. "The crystal. Quick! Hold it above your head. Hurry! We have only a few seconds left."

Instantly, Jeremy realised that it was their only hope. He was so much in a panic that his trembling fingers almost dropped the crystal into the waters of the moat. At last, with shaking hands he lifted the crystal high above his head and, holding their breath the children waited for the magic of the crystal to start working.

Nothing happened. Nothing at all, and the crystal remained dead and lifeless. Jeremy shook the stone, praying for it to help them. He held it high again, but there was still no response.

Then it was all too late. With a final jerk they were lifted over the castle turret, and the next moment they were dropped onto the stony floor. As they looked up they saw the great, terrible shape of the Spiderking towering over them.

"Ha, Ha, Ha!" The creature laughed and jeered at them. "So you thought that you would escape! Ha, Ha, Ha! No one has ever escaped from me, and no one ever will! I have watched every move you have made, even when you did not choose my silver fish that I put in the magic pond. You really thought that silly little crystal would help you against *me*. Ha, Ha, Ha! My magic is made from all the black wickedness in the universe. To imagine that a useless crystal of Peace would be strong enough to overcome it! What nonsense! Ha, Ha, Ha!"

The mocking laughter rang in the children's ears as the Spiderking snatched for the crystal which was still in Jeremy's hand.

Jeremy acted angrily. Without really thinking what he was doing, he threw the crystal directly at the monster and his aim was perfect. Flashing through the air, suddenly alive and glowing, the crystal struck the Spiderking exactly in the middle of its loathsome face. Amazingly, it did not fall away to the floor but seemed to fasten itself firmly against the creature's skin. As it did so a brilliant white glow surrounded it.

The Spiderking shrieked and jumped backwards with an enormous crash. It tried to tear the crystal away, but there was nothing that it could do. The white glow spread and spread across the spider's face and the creature ran madly round and across the room, backwards and forwards, shaking, shrieking, crashing into everything, and all the time scratching and tearing at the crystal, trying to move it away.

Its efforts were useless. The white glow continued to spread. With increasing speed it covered the whole of the Spiderking's head until, with a crash that shook the whole castle, the creature fell to the floor, its legs kicking and waving madly. Still the strange crystal-glow continued to spread. A few more moments, and the entire body was covered. Then, more slowly the legs, one by one, until within just a short space of time every part of the Spiderking was flashing white.

The children were trembling and shivering – not from fright, but from an intensely cold wind which was blowing from the direction of the white-glistening Spiderking. The creature lay spread out on the ground before them. With a last thunderous, frantic crashing from all the sixteen legs the monster was dead.

The children turned and ran as fast as they could from the evil castle, with Twitch scurrying well ahead of them.

As they dashed through the wooden door, now swinging wide open, the castle walls began to shake and grind, and the floor heaved up and down in terrifying waves. Out of the door, across the moat and down the path they dashed.

Then, with cries of fright they skidded to a halt, for there, just ahead of them was a long line of the dreaded, three legged imps, blocking their way completely.

The children stood still. What could they do now? They had thought that, with the destruction of the Spiderking they would be free to go safely, but they had forgotten about the imps, waiting in the darkness of the trees. Their hearts sank as they stood there, shaking with fear.

Just then Jeremy said, "It's strange. Instead of attacking us, the imps are not moving at all."

It was true! The Imps were absolutely still. There was no screaming. There was no waving of Devil-Forks. Just silence.

"Even their eyes are closed." Charlotte said.

The children took a step forward, then another. Still the imps remained as still as statues. Closer and closer the children walked until they were only a foot or two away.

"They are all dead," said Charlotte in a hushed voice. "When the Spiderking was destroyed they must have lost all the evil power that kept them alive!"

Jeremy was peering closely at the imps.

"Yes," he said, "I suppose that's because they were made by the

Spiderking's wicked spells. Now the spells have all been destroyed."

Charlotte reached out and pushed one of the imps until it rocked. Then, with a hard shove, she pushed again, and it fell flat on its face, on the ground. It looked so odd, laying there, with its three feet sticking up in the air.

For the first time in ages, the children laughed heartily. They had a great time rushing up and down the line of unmoving imps, pushing them all over until they lay strewn across the ground, like a hundred oddly shaped, dead tree trunks. As the imps fell, Jeremy grabbed their forks and broke them in half.

As the last one toppled to the ground there came a strange rumbling and grinding, and the ground trembled underfoot.

The three turned just in time to see that the castle was collapsing like a pack of cards. Wide cracks appeared in the great turrets, and massive stones broke away and tumbled onto the walls beneath. Huge gaps split the walls from top to bottom. Slowly the walls began to fall, thundering down to the ground in smoking ruin. It took only a few minutes, and the great castle was no more than a scattered heap of stone, from which a black dust drifted up into the sky. Then that too was gone, carried off by the evening breeze.

The deadly power of the Spiderking was over, the terrible maze was destroyed, and the seventh key was safely in the hands of the children.

And so they began their journey back towards the village of the Machine Children. Twitch, as usual, was dashing on ahead, full of cat-like curiosity. when suddenly the children heard him call, "Meow! Jeremy. Meow! Charlotte."

Twitch came bounding back towards them. He had, shortly before, disappeared over a low sand-bank, and now, after his dash back, he was so much out of breath with excitement that he was unable to say anything more. All he could do was to point . . .

The children looked up in surprise, and ran over to see what he had found. As they came to the top of the sand bank they stopped dead in their tracks, almost unable to believe what they saw. A small river was flowing where, only a few moments before there had been nothing but sand.

It was not so much the river that surprised them. It was mainly the small boat that they saw floating on it. Nothing was holding the boat in place, and the water was flowing fast, but the little boat remained in exactly the same spot, just one step from the river bank.

With one swift jump Twitch landed in the boat, and took up a position right at the very front, where he could see everything that was going on.

Charlotte looked at the boat thoughtfully.

"I'll bet that I know what you're thinking," laughed Jeremy. "We can float down to the village on the boat."

Charlotte nodded. Without further hesitation the children joined Twitch.

Immediately they were all aboard, the boat started to move entirely by itself. Not in the direction of the current, as they had imagined but quite the opposite.

"Oh gosh!" groaned Charlotte, round-eyed with surprise. "Here we go again."

For a while there was silence as the boat steadily moved forwards along the silvery river. Then Jeremy said, "Well, we have all the keys, but we still have to find the land of the Wizard, and the dungeon of the seven doors. Perhaps that's where the power of the keys is leading us!"

Charlotte nodded in agreement, and Twitch gave a loud "Purr" to show that he thought the same. Then he curled up comfortably on a piece of old sacking and closed his eyes. Charlotte felt so tired that she fell asleep even while she was listening to Jeremy. Lulled by the rocking of the boat, he too was soon fast asleep.

The boat floated on and on, throughout the warm night, and the children were still asleep when, with the gentlest of bumps the boat came to a final stop.

FIRE WORLD

As the boat grounded with a quiet "crunch" onto the sandy beach, the children's eyes opened, and they sat up, yawning. The air was hot and dry, and there was a choking smell of burning.

"We'd better get out of the boat," Jeremy said.

Twitch was out first. "Meow!" he went as his paws touched the burning sand.

"I can't imagine where we are now – or why we are here," said Charlotte.

"Don't you remember?" he replied. A long time ago, on Home World, the woodcutter said that the Wizard's castle could be found in the land of fire. This must be where he meant, and so that is why we are here."

Charlotte sniffed. "I can't remember, but you must be right. This is the kind of place that the Wizard would use to guard the castle. He certainly would not wish it to be easy for anyone to get to him."

They both stepped out of the boat and saw that Twitch was still hopping about. His paws were scorching.

"Poor Twitch," she said. "I'll carry you until we get away from this hot sand," and lifting him up, she popped him into the haversack, with only his head poking out.

"Thanks," said the cat, licking his paws. "That was getting very unpleasant. It's alright for you two, you've got shoes on."

"I feel as though I am roasting," Jeremy said. "What are we going to do?"

Charlotte answered at once, "The best thing is to get back into the boat and onto the river again. Then we can float away from this horrid burning place, and perhaps find somewhere better to land."

The children turned back towards the boat – but it had gone. The wide river was now only a small stream which dwindled and narrowed as they watched until, in less than a minute it had totally faded away. Where its sparkling waters had been there remained only the hot, smoking sand. It was hard to believe that it had ever existed.

"We haven't got much choice now," said Jeremy. "No river, and no boat. We'll have to get going, and hope that the smoke and fire will come to an end soon."

The children turned round and peered in every direction, looking for a sign as to which way they should go. However, to North, East, South and West, there was nothing to be seen but the brown, smoking sand. It filled their eyes, throats and noses with its searing smell. There were a few bushes with shrivelled, greyish leaves here and there, but there were no trees, nor grass, nor flowers alive in that poisonous, fiery air. Overhead were thick, yellowish clouds of smoke which blotted out any chance of seeing the sun or moon. All the time wisps of the yellowish smoke drifted downwards, adding to the fumes from the sand, making the children cough and cough, and causing their eyes to stream painfully.

"You must stop rubbing your eyes, Jeremy," Charlotte warned. "You'll only make them worse." She could feel her own eyes itching and smarting as she spoke, and it was all she could do to stop rubbing them, herself.

Again the children peered unhappily around, trying to see through the yellow mists of smoke.

Jeremy broke the silence. "Am I imagining it," he said slowly, "or do you think that the sky looks a little clearer over there?" He lifted his arm and pointed.

Charlotte looked in that direction. She could see no difference in the thick clouds, but she knew that they would have to make a move soon. If she agreed with Jeremy, and pretended to see the clearer patch, it might cheer him up a little, and so she nodded.

"I think you're right," she said, crossing her fingers. "O.K. Let's go."

So, they set off across the clinging sand. Twitch bobbed up and down in the haversack, eyes tightly closed. They plodded on for hours, eyes cast down to avoid the dust and smoke as far as possible. There were long flat patches. There were hard patches where it was easy to walk, and there were soft patches where, with every step, they sank to the ankles in the burning sand. At times they found themselves going up and down, up and down over numbers of steep sand-dunes, and these were the places they hated most. Their throats were too sore, and their tongues too dry for them to speak.

Jeremy trailed along behind Charlotte. His feet were scorched and his eyes hurt so much that he had them almost closed. He was just wondering how much longer he could keep going when, with a bump he walked into Charlotte – just as Twitch had walked into him, in the Spider Maze. Charlotte had suddenly stopped, but when Jeremy walked into her she was pushed forwards so that both children lost their balance. They rolled over and over down a small slope, and were covered, head to foot, by the soft, choking sand.

Twitch jumped crossly from the haversack. He did not like being jolted awake from his comfortable sleep. Stalking angrily over to the children he called out, "Meow. Meow. You should be more careful!"

Charlotte was not listening. She had grasped Jeremy's arm tightly, and was saying, in a strange, quiet voice, "Jeremy. Come back here. Look! Look! Quickly!"

Dragging Jeremy up to the top of the little sand hill, she pointed with a shaking finger. At first he could see nothing through the hazy smoke. Neither could Twitch, who promptly started to moan again.

"Meow. First you drop me, on the ground, rolling me over and over on this horrible sand. Then you get me to rush up this hill, burning my paws. And for what? Just to look at a whole lot of nothing!"

He was going to say a lot more, when suddenly his whiskers stood on end, his fur bristled and his mouth dropped open. He could hardly believe his eyes.

In the distance, the clouds had parted. For a moment, and far away a bright shaft of sunlight shone through the yellow dust like a searchlight. Its golden beam fell upon a wonderful white, shining castle, with windows sparkling and gleaming, reflecting the blue waters of a wide moat that lapped against the great stone walls. A hundred delicate spires and turrets were outlined against the sky. From the tallest turret of all there floated a brilliant, many-coloured flag.

"It must be the castle of the seven doors," Charlotte said.

Jeremy quickly added, "You mean the Wizard's castle? The castle with the dungeon of the seven doors!"

He could understand how Charlotte had got her words mixed up. In the wonder of that moment he too had difficulty in speaking.

As if a curtain had fallen, the light was gone and once more the beautiful castle was lost from sight behind the clouds of smoky dust.

With the memory of it bright in their minds, giving them renewed hope and strength, the children set off again. There was a difference now. They were no longer just wandering *anywhere*! This time they knew exactly what direction to take.

They continued on their way over the unfriendly, burning desert. For the rest of that day they marched ever onwards, talking with excitement about the castle that they had seen so briefly.

"How can the Wizard be so bad?" wondered Charlotte, out loud, "and yet live in such a beautiful place?"

Jeremy had been thinking almost the same thoughts. It was really quite a puzzle – one that, as yet, had no answer.

"Things aren't always exactly as they seem," he replied after a while. "Perhaps we'll find that the castle is completely different when we get close enough to see it clearly."

And so it was with thoughts such as these, filling their minds, that they trudged on and on until, as evening drew near, the shadows lengthened and the light began to fade. For some time Charlotte had been looking around for some form of shelter to spend the night. There was a small hollow in the ground, surrounded by the greyish bushes. It looked a good place to rest safely. As she turned to point it out to Jeremy, with no warning, darkness fell upon them, a darkness so black that the children could not see anything at all.

Charlotte reached out to touch Jeremy's shoulder, and the two children half stumbled, and half fell down into the small, sandy hollow. The sand was soft and the air remained warm. The children were so tired that, despite the unpleasant smokiness they were asleep almost at once, hardly moving at all as the night slowly passed and the yellowish light of day gradually returned.

There was no change in their surroundings next morning. The air was still just as hot, and the wisps of smoke still floated making them cough, and making their eyes hurt. The clouds were still as thick overhead – everything was the same. Or was it?

Jeremy felt that something was wrong the moment he opened his eyes. "Wake up! Wake up!" he cried as he shook Charlotte's arm.

Surprised, Charlotte sat up, rubbing her eyes. "What is it? Are we being attacked?"

"Oh no, Charlotte," Jeremy replied. "It's worse than that. It's Twitch. He's gone."

The children hunted and searched everywhere. Under all the bushes, until they were covered in scratches from the dry, prickly leaves. Behind the rocks, and for yards and yards around, up and down the sand hills and into every hollow. All with no success, for there was no sign of Twitch at all. They called and they called until their throats were so sore that they could not make another sound, but there was no reply. Only the silence of the desert mocked them when they stood and listened.

"Do you think we'll ever see our Twitch again?" Jeremy whispered.

Charlotte had no answer. She had been thinking the same thing, but didn't want to admit it. Instead, she said, "Don't be so silly. Of course we'll find him. I know exactly what we must do."

"What?"

"We must first go back up to the top of the sand hill, where we were last night before we fell down into the hollow. Then we'll hunt very, very carefully for Twitch's footprints. The sand is soft and we'll be able to see, quite clearly, in which direction he went. All we have to do is to follow the footprints and we'll find him. It will be quite easy, you'll see."

The plan sounded so sensible that Jeremy cheered up immediately. In fact, it sounded so sensible to Charlotte, as she

149

spoke, that she even felt quite a bit happier. So, climbing up through the bushes, the two children once again stood on the level sand, finding their footprints of the night before without difficulty.

"Look!" said Jeremy. "Here are our footprints. See how they lead down through the bushes, and that big scuffed place is where we fell over. But where are Twitch's paw marks?"

"You search for them across that side," Charlotte replied, "and I will hunt around over here. In no way must we lose sight of each other, even for one second, or we may all get lost!"

So they started to search for some trace of their lost friend. First up, then down. Straight and across. Then up and down again. There was nothing to be seen, and it was all beginning to seem a hopeless task when Jeremy shouted out in happy excitement.

"Here! Here! Quick, Charlotte. These must be Twitch's prints. It looks as though he wandered round and round in the dark, trying to find his way back to us before setting off this way."

Jeremy pointed to where the paw-prints crossed and re-crossed themselves several times before leading away into the gloom.

"Oh, poor old Twitch," said Charlotte sadly. "He must be lost and feeling really terrified."

With all haste the children followed the faint marks in the sand as they went up and down the small hills and through the dry, scrubby bushes. The tracks wandered everywhere, doubled back and crossed from one side to another, showing how Twitch had searched and searched in vain for the children. All morning Jeremy and Charlotte followed the small paw-marks until, with blistered feet, and arms and legs scratched in a dozen places by the rough bushes, they sank to the ground, exhausted.

Jeremy lay on his back, arms outstretched watching the clouds of smoke as they thickened and thinned overhead. The gloomy, dust-filled air stopped the children from seeing very far in any direction. However, as the clouds thinned for a brief moment, Charlotte noticed a shimmering gleam, over to the side, at the foot of a small hill.

"What's that?" she cried out, and jumped to her feet. Together, the children pushed their way through the grey bushes to get a closer look. As they burst through the last and thickest of the bushes they came to a sudden halt. They held their breaths. What lay before them was the last thing they ever expected to see on this dry, burning world. There, at their feet, stretching several yards across, was a small lake, black as ink, somehow frightening in its total stillness.

The children just stood and stared, not daring to approach closer. The lake was like a mirror, with not the faintest ripple nor wave disturbing its glassy surface. Strange wisps of the yellow clouds floated across it, twisting like menacing ghosts.

Charlotte broke the silence with a small cry. "There they are!" she called out. "Jeremy, there they are!"

"There *what* are?" Jeremy asked crossly. Charlotte had quite frightened him when she called out, and he had no idea what she was talking about.

"Twitch's paw-marks. Can't you see?" Charlotte said. "They lead directly to the edge of the water. He must be somewhere near here!"

The tracks lead directly to the water – but there they stopped. There were no tracks coming back, and none the other side. It was as though the cat had jumped in, and disappeared.

"What happened to Twitch?" wondered Jeremy?

"I don't know," said Charlotte. "I can't see anything in this lake."

They both looked more carefully.

"There!" Charlotte cried out. "There is something floating on the surface."

"I can see it," said Jeremy. "It's Twitch's red bow, from his collar."

"We must reach for it," said Charlotte.

"But the water looks terrible," Jeremy said, frightened.

"I know, but we must find Twitch. This is our only clue," said Charlotte.

"I'll go," said a very determined Jeremy. With a small smile at Charlotte, and with the greatest of care he put one foot into the water.

It was icy cold. As the water touched his leg he felt an odd, electric tingle run through his body. Then he gasped in surprise, for the lake which had looked so deep and dangerous was amazingly shallow, and the water barely came to his knees as he slowly paddled towards the red bow.

"I'm coming as well," Charlotte said; together they reached the spot where the bow still floated.

Then everything happened at once. Jeremy reached towards the bow, Charlotte screamed and seized hold of his arm. The ground moved beneath their feet. In a split second they found themselves falling, falling down a brightly lit, and completely round hole, to land with a crash on a great heap of dry, spiky leaves which must have come from the desert bushes, now so high above.

Still clutching the haversack safely, Charlotte sprang to her feet.

"Where are we?" Jeremy said, standing up and shaking the leaves off his clothes.

The children looked eagerly around their new surroundings. The very first thing they noticed, to their great relief, was that the air was clear and free from smoke or dust, and at last they could breathe again without choking. The place was oddly shaped, almost round but with a number of squared sides.

"It reminds me of something," Jeremy said, and he thought hard, trying to remember what it was.

Charlotte moved across to the nearest wall which was almost transparent and pressed her face as close as she could. Through the glassy bricks she could see the blurred outlines of hundreds of similar rooms, all joined together and spreading outwards and onwards. She then looked down, towards the floor. It was the same, with room after room all the same odd shape fading away into the distance. She looked upwards. Just as she was beginning to expect there were more of the strange rooms, countless numbers of them, in every direction.

Then Jeremy cried out, "I know where we are!"

"Where?"

"In a giant bee-hive," he said importantly.

"You're right," Charlotte said, looking around.

Jeremy continued his explanation, "These hundreds of rooms all around us are the empty cells, waiting to be filled with young bees, or honey, or something. We have to get out before the bees come back. They must be huge. They might think that we're just the right size to feed to the little bees."

"The hidden entrance must be to keep the dust out," said Charlotte. "We must find the way out now."

Frantically, the two children searched for an exit. There had to be a doorway somewhere, that the bees themselves used, but where was it?

"There," said Charlotte, pointing to a crack in the glassy walls. It was so fine it was almost invisible, and so thin that, no matter how hard they tried they could not even get their finger-nails into it to pull the door open.

"It's useless," said Jeremy.

Sitting back on their heels the children studied the doorway afresh. Inch by inch they examined its surface, and then, just as it seemed they would find nothing new they saw it – a tiny hole only just above the surface of the floor. It had to be some form of keyhole, but what use was that going to be, without the right key to fit it? Time was passing and the children knew that, at any moment the bees might come back, and so their fear and agitation grew stronger.

Hot and bothered, Charlotte dropped the haversack down on the floor beside her, and as she did so she heard a faint "clink" from inside. Suddenly she jumped to her feet again, and said in a shaking voice,

"Jeremy, perhaps one of the seven keys will help! Remember, they are full of magic!"

"I'm not sure we should even try," Jeremy said.

"But if we don't escape from here the keys won't be of any use to us at all," Charlotte replied.

Jeremy nodded slowly. "Alright then," he said.

Charlotte hastily unfastened the little package which she had hidden deep within the haversack, and she placed the seven wonderful keys before her.

"They all seem too big for the keyhole," Charlotte said. "I don't think they can help at all."

The two gazed at the line of keys, each won after so much hardship. There was the golden key from Home World. No. That was so obviously the wrong shape that she soon put it carefully away.

"What about the jewelled key from Ice World?" whispered Jeremy. "It looks as though its the right shape."

Charlotte shook her head. The jewels stuck out so much from the

153

side that it had no chance of getting into the small round keyhole. She put that one away, too.

"The silver key from the World of Air?" Jeremy asked.

"The jewel key from the Golden Castle?" Charlotte wondered.

"The glass key from the Machine Children?" Jeremy said, picking it up.

"Or the stone key from Spider Maze?" Charlotte asked.

No. Jeremy and Charlotte shook their heads. Not one of the keys was suitable. It was hard to believe that all these beautiful keys of magic were of no use. Charlotte sadly packed them away.

"There's still one missing," Jeremy said.

Charlotte reached for the last one – the rough wooden key from Underground. She had not even considered that one. "It looks so unsuitable," she said. It was large and roughly made, and was completely the wrong shape. "But it feels strange. It's warm."

"Look," said Jeremy. "It's changing."

Round the tip of the key, there had appeared a faint, blue, shimmering light. As the children stared, the light grew brighter and fiercer until it was a tiny ball of brilliance. It burned steadily without a flicker. Despite its brightness, it did not hurt the children's eyes. As Charlotte lifted the key in the air the fire remained perfectly balanced at the tip.

Slowly, and with delicate care, Charlotte turned towards the glassy door, bringing the wooden key forwards and then down to the tiny key-hole.

"What'll happen now?" she asked. "The key's too big for the key-hole."

"Let's wait and see," Jeremy replied.

There was not a sound in that strange room of glass as the magic began to work. The blue flame lifted from the key and floated towards the key-hole. Closer and closer. Just as it almost touched, there was a flash of incredible brilliance, as if the sun itself had come into the room. The blue light seemed to fill the crack which outlined the door. For only the smallest space of time it flared, and then with a rushing, roaring sound – it was gone.

And as it disappeared, the glass door swung open wide.

Just a few paces forward, then the children paused anxiously in the doorway, for who knows what they might have found?

"Phew! It's empty," Jeremy said, relieved.

Ahead was a wide, long hall with the walls, floor and ceiling all made from hundreds more of the empty, waiting cells. The same pearly light that had lit the entrance room glimmered ahead and around them. At the far end of the hallway a brighter, golden glow seemed to promise a return to sunlight and the open air.

As Charlotte and Jeremy stepped through the doorway and into the glass-like hall, the door clicked shut behind them.

"We can only go forwards, now," Charlotte said. "Towards the sunlight."

"It doesn't seem too far away," Jeremy said.

"But we have to be quick in case the bees come back," Charlotte reminded him.

The hallway had many unexpected twists and turns, and it went up and down. On and on it stretched, and it seemed to have no end. But the golden glow appeared to be getting no closer.

"This must be the way Twitch came," Jeremy said. "There's no other way, but I cannot imagine how he got through the glass door."

"I'm looking forward to hearing his explanation," Charlotte said, (but, somehow, she never did find the answer). Then she was interrupted by Jeremy' shout.

"Hey! Something's changing here." Indeed, the empty cells around them were becoming less transparent and were taking on a darker, golden colour. A glowing light was reflecting from the walls ahead. As they walked steadily forward the glow, now golden, like the cells, grew stronger.

Suddenly, Charlotte stopped.

"Listen," she said. "Do you hear that?"

Jeremy had already heard the noise, faintly at first but becoming louder as they approached a sharp bend. There was a huge rock which stopped them from seeing round. As they came right up to it, the noise became very, very loud. It was a humming, whirring sound.

"Bees!" Charlotte shouted.

Before them was a most startling scene. The hallway had come to an end, leading into a high, domed cave which opened into the outer world. Through this opening the sunlight streamed. But also through the opening flew dozens of giant bees. The air was full of them, all in continuous movement. Their coloured fur gleamed in the bright sunshine.

For a while the children watched silently, fascinated by the incredible picture in front of them. The bees were in three different colours. Some were blue and yellow, some green and yellow and some red and yellow. They all seemed to have different jobs. The activity was unending.

"The different colours must mean different kinds of bees," Charlotte said.

"Yes," agreed Jeremy.

Those with the green bands flew out through the opening into the sunlight and returned later, laden with all kinds of strange objects, and with their legs heavy with thick, clinging pollen. The children watched as the bees crawled down the hallway opposite, brushing the pollen into the empty cells.

"It means that soon the Queen'll arrive to fill the cells with eggs," Charlotte explained, trying to remember hard what she had learned long ago.

"Gosh," said Jeremy. "Thank goodness they didn't start over on this side. We'd never have been able to get past them."

"And we might not, yet!" said Charlotte grimly to herself. "Unless we find a way out through them."

Jeremy's attention was on the other bees. "I think that the blue ones are the lazy ones," he said. "They don't seem to work at all. They just buzz around stealing the pollen from the others."

"And getting in the way of the other bees," added Charlotte. "But what are the red bees up to?" she wondered.

She was not long left in doubt. Suddenly the outside entrance was blocked by an enormous head. An enormous, horny leg, then another, and another, scrabbled through, trying to break the sides of the cave to make room for its body to enter. There was a terrible noise of crashing and grinding from the crumbling rocks. The red bees seemed to be gathering in their hundreds in the centre of the cave, making even more noise.

"I can see now," shrieked Jeremy, jumping up and down in

excitement. "It's a huge ant!"

Charlotte quickly put her hand over his mouth to keep him quiet. "I don't want the bees to find us now," she said.

A small army of the red bees zoomed across the cave and threw themselves fiercely against the giant ant's head, twisting and turning, spinning in all directions in their attempts to get their stings into a soft place. The great black legs of the ant swung up and across, crushing several of the bees to the ground. But, as fast as they were knocked down, more came to take up the fight, darting and stinging the invading monster. At last, with bellows of rage and pain, the ant fled.

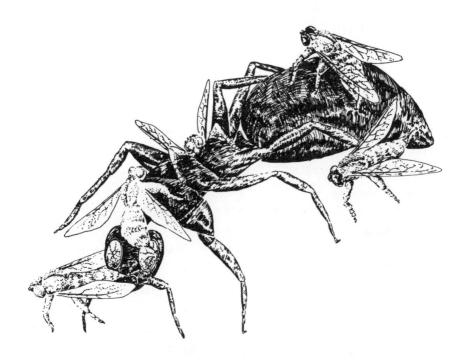

Silence fell over the great cave. For a moment it seemed as if time stood still. Then, in an explosion of activity, the green bees started to rush around, buzzing and whirring as they began the task of clearing up, mending the broken walls and carrying away the bees that had been killed. There were so many bees to do the work that it was not very long before the job was done. Soon there was no trace left of the dreadful fight that had taken place in front of the children.

Then, as if nothing had happened, the green bees returned to their work, flying in and out of the cave and returning laden with pollen. The busy scene was back to normal.

Jeremy and Charlotte continued to look around and watched everything carefully.

"I wonder why, now and again, one of the Bees flies off to that dark corner," Jeremy said, pointing towards a far corner of the cave.

"Well, I don't think they're taking any pollen there," Charlotte replied. "They're just carrying berries, nuts, small fruits – and, look, there's a dead grasshopper!"

"We must find out why," said Jeremy. "Come this way," he whispered. "If there is something strange about that corner, it might be to do with Twitch."

The two children began to creep quietly across. There were many great piles of rock for them to hide behind. They moved only when it seemed that the bees were looking elsewhere. So, without being seen, they finally reached the other side.

The floor was littered with all the odd bits and pieces which they had seen the bees carrying.

"The smell is terrible," Charlotte said wrinkling her nose in disgust.

But she didn't have much time to think about it, as Jeremy cried out, "Charlotte, look!"

"Something's moving in the shadow," Charlotte confirmed.

The children jumped backwards, falling over each other in their fright. As they did so, a voice spoke from the darkness.

"Meow, Meow, Meow. Where have you been? You've taken long enough to find me!" It was the most welcome sound that they had heard for a long time. Twitch strolled forward, tail straight in the air.

"Sometime, I want to know exactly what you've been up to," said Charlotte. "But not here and now. First, we must find our way out from this place."

The three of them sat down, well-hidden, and discussed a dozen ideas for escape. But each idea was full of problems. An hour later they were still without any kind of plan.

"There is only one way out, and that is through the

cave entrance."

The others nodded in agreement.

"Can we get through with the Cloak of Invisibility?" asked Jeremy.

"No, because there are so many bees, rushing in all directions," Charlotte explained. "We would bump into them, and then we would soon be caught"

Both Jeremy and Twitch nodded gloomily. Once again there was silence as they were all lost in their own thoughts. Their minds buzzed endlessly with plans and ideas, but none of them seemed to make any sense. Long into the afternoon they sat there, speaking only the odd word and with a feeling of defeat slowly surrounding them. Twitch, worn out with all the events of the day, fell asleep at their feet.

The shadows were growing longer and evening was almost upon them. The light began to fade. As its last sun rays slanted through the cave entrance, Charlotte suddenly sat upright and stared across to where the bees were still bustling around.

"I think there are fewer bees now," she said.

Together, Jeremy and Charlotte tried to count them, but the bees were moving about too much.

"No, I know what's happening," she said, shaking her head. "The bees are still flying back in, but they're not flying out."

As the minutes passed, fewer and fewer bees returned. Finally, as darkness was complete, the air grew quiet and still.

"They're going to sleep now," Jeremy said.

"This is our chance to escape," Charlotte said.

Jeremy was already on his feet when Charlotte said, "Now."

"Now," Jeremy repeated, nudging Twitch awake with his foot.

"Now!" they all said together. Very quietly and with no further delay they tip-toed quickly across the cave.

It all seemed so easy. With no difficulty, and in absolute silence, they stepped through the entrance. At last they were back in the open air.

Around them was a wide, flat field of grass. They ran as fast as they could until the cave of the bees was far behind. Then they sank to the ground, completely worn out. A fresh breeze blew all the last traces of smoke and dust away from their clothes and hair.

The air was sweet and clean and the sky so clear.

"The world has changed again," Charlotte said.

Jeremy and Twitch were already asleep.

THE SEVEN DOORS

The sun was high when they awoke the next day. The sky was clear, and blue.

"We must be close to the white castle," Charlotte said as she stood up.

Twitch stretched and rolled on the soft grass. The bushes and trees were green – and there were even birds singing.

"No more burning sands," said Jeremy as he sat up.

His thoughts were interrupted by Charlotte's cry of "Look! Jeremy! I can see the castle!"

"Where?" asked Jeremy, looking around him.

"Stand up and you'll be able to see," Charlotte replied.

Jeremy jumped to his feet.

"Let's go," he said, "Quickly, come on!"

"Wait," said Charlotte, "How do we know if this is the Wizard's castle?"

"It's just got to be," said Jeremy, and Twitch nodded.

"I agree," he purred. "There can't be any other castles like that."

Charlotte, Jeremy and Twitch walked across the grass in the warm sunshine, hardly daring to let their hopes rise too high. At last they stood by the silver waters of the moat.

"There's something wrong again," said Charlotte. "I can feel it."

"No, there isn't," said Jeremy. "Let's go. We have to find our way across, and into the castle – there must be a bridge and a door. Let's look!"

Along the side of the moat they walked, comfortable in the fresh, clear air, picking their way between small bushes, looking at the flowers and scrambling over low fences which, here and there, divided the fields. But there was no bridge, and no boat floated on the quiet water.

"We've walked all the way round," said Jeremy, looking worried.

"We'll have to think hard," said Charlotte. "Really, it's ridiculous! Here's the castle. The Wizard and all his servants live inside. They *must* be able to get in and out, so therefore there has to be some kind of door. "

Jeremy nodded as he replied. "Well, if there *is* a door, we should have seen it. Why didn't we?"

As he spoke, he took off his shoes and paddled his feet in the water, sending silver ripples lapping against the castle walls. "What are we going to do next, Char . . ." He stopped talking as he saw a curious object sticking out from the ground, just above the water, beside his toes. Half to himself he said, "Funny. What's this?" The object was directly under the grassy bank on which he sat, and was quite impossible to see unless you knew it was there.

Jeremy bent forward to look more closely, and saw that it was a bright, shining ring of metal. It was fastened onto a large stone slab, set into the side of the moat. It was just within his reach, and he could not resist the urge to bend over, and give it a gentle tug.

Everything then happened very quickly. The stone moved easily – so easily, that Jeremy lost his balance and fell downwards through the small, square opening that had appeared.

Charlotte had not seen any of this happen. She had been leaning back in the grass, with her eyes closed, puzzling over the castle with no doors. Therefore, when she spoke to Jeremy next, and received no answer, she was quite annoyed.

"Where are you?" she called. "Jeremy, where have you gone?"

At first she thought that he may have fallen into the water, but she had heard no splash. She called out, again and again, and now Twitch was also calling, and joining her in searching under every bush and looking into every tree.

"He can't be here," Charlotte said. But there was nowhere else to look. She sat down and thought hard.

Jeremy found himself lying flat on his face in a wide, brightly lit room. Behind him, in absolute silence, the stone slab slid shut. He could faintly hear Charlotte calling. He tugged and tugged at the stone door in a useless attempt to make it open. Several minutes of panic-filled struggling passed before he realised that *pulling* was not the answer. It was quite by accident that he gave the slightest of *pushes* that made the stone swing open wide, just above the level of the water. He pushed his head and shoulders through, carefully holding the stone slab open with one hand.

"Charlotte, I'm here," he called out loudly. "I'm down here."

Charlotte turned round and round. She could hear his voice but could not see him anywhere.

"Where are you?" she shouted, "I can't see you. I wish you wouldn't go away like that."

"Sorry, Charlotte," replied Jeremy. "It really *was* an accident. Come over here, by the water, and look down."

Charlotte and Twitch ran across to the side of the moat, from where they had heard Jeremy's voice. Looking down, they saw Jeremy's head sticking out from the stone doorway.

"Quickly!" said Jeremy. "It's hard to hold the door open. Jump in!"

Without a moment's hesitation, Charlotte picked Twitch up and jumped down beside Jeremy who let go of the stone slab. As before, it closed silently, shutting out the sun, the moat and the castle.

The room the children stood in was bright but empty of any kind of furniture. A wide corridor, full of strange, reflecting lights stretched away in front of them. Its curved floor and walls ended on a curved roof.

"I feel as if I am standing in a long tube," Charlotte commented.

"So do I," said Jeremy.

The stone slabs forming the walls were blood-red, those on the floor a vivid green, and in the brilliant lighting the colours were harsh and menacing.

"Ugh!" said Jeremy. "It's so ugly!"

"Never mind," said Charlotte. "This must be the secret entrance we've been looking for."

As they continued along their way, the hard colours made their eyes ache. At first they did not notice that the lights were getting dimmer and the floor was, very slightly, sloping upwards. The air grew colder and still the lights continued to fade.

As they turned another bend, they saw, blocking the way in front of them, a great, iron-barred door. Jet-black, it reached high above their heads into the shadows. It fitted closely to the floor, roof and walls and was covered by thick, draping cob-webs. Large, beady eyes of hundreds of spiders watched them hungrily. The children stopped dead in their tracks.

"One of the keys must unlock it," said Jeremy.

"I know," Charlotte replied, "but I don't want to get near the spiders."

"Never mind the spiders," said a very brave Jeremy. "I don't want to go near them either, but I want to open the door."

Guarding the key-hole closely was a cluster of huge, green spiders, covered with stiff hair. Their enormous, cruel eyes watched every move the children made.

Charlotte took the seven keys out of the haversack.

"I know which one is the right one for *this* door," Jeremy said. The key-hole was large, very large. There was only one key big enough to fit it. "It has to be the rough wooden one. The one we found in the Underground World."

Charlotte bent down and took the wooden key in her hand. "It's warm, just like last time," she said.

Charlotte looked down at the key, and then back to the door covered in spiders and webs. As she did so, a strange feeling took hold of her. As if in a dream, she slowly raised the key until it was high above her head, pointing towards the door. Just as had happened in the hive of the giant bees, a blue ball of fire gathered around the tip of the key. It flickered and glowed brighter and brighter, throwing strange shadows on walls and roof and across the giant door. All was silent.

The spiders stirred uneasily. Charlotte lowered her arm and pointed the key towards the layers and folds of dusty cobwebs. The blue flame now glowed like a small sun. Neither of the children, nor the spiders could take their eyes from it. Suddenly, with a soundless flash, the flame leaped across the gap towards the door.

The silence was broken. With an enormous crash, the webs

exploded into roaring fire and the door was hidden behind a vast sheet of yellow flame. The heat was so intense that the children jumped back several paces. Twitch went scurrying half-way back along the corridor. Soon nothing could be seen but a dense, swirling fog of black smoke.

As suddenly as it had started, the fire stopped. The smoke began to twist into nothingness and once more there was deep silence. Where the webs and the spiders had been, there were now only a few blackened threads and a heap of fine, dusty ash.

Holding the wooden key in her hand, Charlotte reached out and placed it in the keyhole through which the golden light was still pouring. As she did so, she hastily drew back her arm with a small cry of fright, for the key had seemed to twist in her fingers. The key slowly turned by itself, and the massive door swung open.

There was the sound of a great bell striking one booming stroke, then all was silence again.

Jeremy was the first to move. With a shout of excitement he bounded through the doorway and into the room beyond, onto a floor of enormous stone slabs.

"Look," he said, pointing at the centre of the room.

There stood a gigantic stone image. From its bright yellow eyes came the light they had seen through the key-hole.

"This looks very much like more trouble," said Charlotte.

The glowing eyes in the stone face seemed to fasten upon the children, and the great mouth seemed to twist in a horrible smile.

"Look at his arms," Charlotte said.

All over the huge stone body grew branch-like arms which ended in thin, skeleton-like claws. The arms waved and twisted ceaselessly, as if eager to grasp any living thing foolish enough to come within their reach.

"And look at that," said Jeremy, pointing at where the arms were at their thickest. "A door!"

"It's the second door," said Charlotte.

"We'll have to get through," said Jeremy.

"Let's get closer," Charlotte continued. "We may be able to see if there is a safe way past those arms."

The children advanced to within a few feet of the eager claws. At that point, the monster went completely mad. Its eyes flashed and glared, and its mouth twisted into horrible shapes. Its arms shook wildly and thrashed about, reaching and grasping at the air, trying to stretch far enough out to capture the children.

Jeremy and Charlotte were now so close that they could see the door clearly. It was of grey stone, and had a mark in the exact centre.

"That must be the keyhole," exclaimed Charlotte. "How can we reach it safely?"

Jeremy started to prowl round the room, exploring every corner, and then, from the far side, he called out, "Hey, come and look at this. Do you think it might be of help to us?"

As Charlotte ran to see what he had found, she saw that he was holding two large pieces of rock, taken from a large pile which lay heaped against the walls.

"If we can break the eyes, the monster won't be able to see where we are," he said excitedly. "And then we can dodge the arms."

Charlotte thought hard. "It may work," she said. "But it may also make things worse if it gets more angry."

"Let's try," said Jeremy.

"Alright. I'll have a go," said Charlotte.

"I'll have a go too," said Jeremy.

"We better make a heap of rocks first," said Charlotte.

"As close as we dare," said Jeremy excitedly.

Soon there was an enormous heap of stones almost in the middle of the room. Holding one rock in each hand, Charlotte took careful aim at the great glaring eyes. Crash! It fell short by several feet. She tried again. Crash! Closer, but it was well over to the side. A third time, a fourth, but no better at all, and the yellow eyes seemed to be laughing at her efforts.

"Let me have a go," Jeremy said.

"Not yet," Charlotte cried. She tried over and over again and missed almost every time. The rocks that *did* hit parts of the stone body fell harmlessly to the ground. The only effect was that the arms squirmed and waved more violently, and the ugly mouth stretched and twisted into worse ugly shapes.

At long last, Jeremy could contain his impatience no longer. "For goodness sake, let me try," he said.

"O.K." Charlotte was quite glad to agree this time. Her arms ached.

Searching through the pile of rocks, Jeremy took one that felt comfortable in his hand. With great care he hurled it at the glaring eyes. It seemed that, even at his first attempt, he was going to score a hit. But, at the last moment, he saw with disappointment that it had fallen a few inches short. Jeremy chose another stone and shifted slightly to the side. Up went his arm! The rock sailed swiftly through the air – was it going to miss again? No. No. NO! With a "thud" it struck one of the glaring eyes straight in the centre.

At first there appeared to be no effect.

167

"Perhaps it was too small," Jeremy said.

"Maybe the eye is too strong," added Charlotte.

Just then a hideous roar came from the wide, gaping mouth of the monster and it began to open and close in raging fury. Its arms thrashed the air, reaching and straining in their maddened attempts to get at the attackers. The glaring lights in the eyes flashed on and off. Dimmer! Brighter! Dimmer! Brighter! With a soundless explosion, the eye that had been struck seemed to collapse inwards, and its horrible glow finally faded to become dark and black.

By this time, Charlotte had placed a small heap of stones by Jeremy's feet. Searching carefully, he took hold of the largest and smoothest one and turned to take aim again. Charlotte stepped back to get out of his way.

"Help!" she cried. In a split second, disaster struck. Charlotte had forgotten the bigger pile of rocks behind her. She tripped, lost her balance and she fell forwards – right into the clutching arms of the stone monster.

In an instance she was being dragged, screaming and struggling towards the grinning, toothless mouth which now opened wide to draw her in.

There was only one way that Jeremy could save her.

Hastily, he picked up one of the stones scattered around his feet and took careful aim. As the stone sailed through the air he held his breath, hardly daring to look.

He need not have doubted, for his aim was perfect. At the very moment that the huge mouth opened its widest and was about to swallow Charlotte, the stone struck the remaining eye with all the force of Jeremy's desperation. The eye opened hugely and its light flared crimson red. It began to open and close rapidly, seeming to twist round in every possible way. From the evil mouth came a deafening, rasping roar which shook the walls of the great cave, and brought showers of rocks tumbling down from all directions.

And then, as before, the blazing light switched off and now both eyes were dark and cold.

The whole of the enormous cave dimmed and became full of shadows. It was so dark that Jeremy could no longer see what was happening to Charlotte. Had she escaped from the terrible claws or did they still clutch her tightly? Cautiously he moved closer to the stone monster until he could, once more see its frightening shape looming through the shadows. Its arms now hung lifelessly by its side and Charlotte was sprawled on the ground.

"Are you alright?" asked Jeremy ,as he dashed across to her.

"Yes," she said, rising to her feet still trembling with fear.

"It's all over," said Jeremy. "The monster's dead."

With some difficulty Charlotte stepped forward and looked back at the monster's body. Twitch came up to her and rubbed his head against her leg.

"How are you?" Jeremy asked in a worried voice, but all Charlotte said was, "Come on. Let's go."

The children walked very slowly, until they stood in front of the small stone door.

"You know," Charlotte said thoughtfully, "The door is stone. The head is stone. The body is stone. Now we are so close we can see that the arms, too were made of stone, and the eyes were really two great searchlights."

"What does it mean?" Jeremy asked.

"This wasn't a living monster. It was only a robot, built to frighten and destroy anyone trying to enter the door."

Twitch gave a "Meow" and said proudly, "We beat it though, didn't we?" Jeremy and Charlotte smiled and nodded.

Charlotte reached into the haversack. She knew that there was no need to search through the keys. She had known, from the moment she had first seen the door, which key would fit. It had to be the smooth, stone key from Spider Maze. One small step forward and she was close enough to try the key in the lock.

With not the slightest fuss or bother the key turned, and the door was open.

Far, far away it seemed, the great bell boomed. Once! Twice! The sound echoed through the room.

As the children stepped through the small doorway they found that it was so small that they could only pass through one at a time.

It was so very low that they had to stoop almost double to avoid banging their heads on the rough, stone roof. Inside, the darkness was almost complete.

At first, the children could see nothing. Gradually they began to make out shapes around them. As their eyes became more used to the darkness, they discovered that they were in a small, stone room. It was completely round and had no windows or doors, except the one they had just passed through. There was no trace of any way out, no corridor nor hallway to lead them on their way, and no stairs going up or down.

Charlotte turned round to examine the room again. "Something's wrong," she said, frowning.

Just then, Jeremy called out, "The door's gone! The door we came through has disappeared."

"We're trapped!" Charlotte cried.

Jeremy and Twitch slowly walked around, examining every inch of the walls, feeling for a crack, a mark, anything to show where the door had been.

"There's nothing," said Jeremy. "It's as if the door had never existed."

The air was becoming hot and stuffy, for the room was so small. With every moment it was getting worse.

"We must find some way out quickly," warned Charlotte, "Or we'll suffocate."

All three examined every hole and crack in the walls again. But that only confirmed that the walls were solid and unbroken. Jeremy walked backwards and forwards across the floor, looking for a trapdoor, but there was no sign of any break in the stone paving. Twitch helped in the search, walking around, sniffing and pawing at every lump and bump, no matter how tiny. But he found nothing and finally gave up and sat quietly against the wall, green eyes glowing in the dim light.

Charlotte was becoming more and more worried. "We can't have escaped the stone monster just to walk straight into a trap," she said.

"Surely not," said Jeremy. "The stone key would never have fitted if we weren't supposed to come this way."

Just then Twitch started making an odd, funny little noise, half "purr" half "meow". It was the kind of noise he always made when he was too excited to speak. Jeremy and Charlotte turned quickly to look at him, and they saw that his eyes were fixed upon something above their heads. Following the direction in which he was staring, they saw, floating in the air, a perfectly round "something".

There was no other way to describe it. Like nothing the children had ever seen before, it seemed to be a circle of light that slowly turned round and round, changing colour the whole time. First a pale, rosy glow, which faded into a deep blue like the summer sky. Then there came a flash of yellow before an emerald green. The green reminded the children of the Fountain of Happiness. All the time the colours changed from light to dark. And all the time they seemed to send a welcome to the three travellers.

The circle of light was far above the children's heads. It was much too high for them to be able to reach, but it had to be a sign, pointing the way to go.

"We must get close to it," Charlotte said. "I'm sure it'll show us the way to the next doorway."

For a moment she stood frowning in thought. Then, opening the haversack, she looked at the five remaining keys. How could she possibly choose the correct one for this incredible doorway of light?

"There doesn't seem to be a key-hole," remarked Charlotte.

The children sat down with the keys laid out before them. Twitch once again started to prowl impatiently around the room and Jeremy leaned back, gazing up at the circle of light. Suddenly an idea came flashing through his mind. Quickly he sprang to his feet, nudging Charlotte with his foot.

"I know," he said excitedly. "Look, that *is* the only doorway out from this cave. But it is nothing like a real door. That is why there is no keyhole. It doesn't work that way. I think that the magic of the right key, when close enough will send a signal that will allow us to enter."

"You're probably right," said Charlotte. "But how can we get close enough to try? The doorway, or whatever it is, is much too high over our heads."

Jeremy smiled. "It's quite simple really. Come over here, underneath the doorway. I'll bend over and you can climb on my

171

back and try each key in turn."

"I'm not too sure," Charlotte replied, but she did as Jeremy asked. He was standing exactly under the circle of light, and as she walked across to him he bent over. Without a further thought she jumped lightly onto his back. Wobbling and almost falling, she stretched upwards, straining towards the glowing ring. Still wobbling she raised herself onto the tips of her toes.

"Hooray! I can reach it," she cried. Her fingers almost touched the shimmering colours.

"Twitch, Twitch," she called. "Please bring me the keys, one by one."

Twitch picked up the golden key in his mouth and bounded over to her. Standing on his back legs, and leaning against Jeremy, his head was just within Charlotte's reach. She took the key gently from Twitch's mouth and carefully held it up towards the light. There was no response. It could not be the correct key. Charlotte handed it down to the cat.

Twitch came back by her side with the silver key. Again Charlotte tested it against the flashing circle. Again, nothing!

"Hurry up, please," groaned Jeremy. "I can't hold you much longer. My back is really aching."

Before he had finished speaking, Twitch had rushed back and had put the silver key away. Then, with the greatest of care he picked up the delicate jewelled key and placed it in Charlotte's hand. Holding her breath she stretched upwards, feeling that, at any moment she was going to lose her balance and fall. And that's exactly what happened.

The children found themselves rolling across the floor. When they came to a stop, and looked upwards they were so amazed that they were quite unable to move.

A wonderful change had started to take place when Charlotte placed the jewelled key near the mysterious circle. Instantly the lights changed colour, flashing even faster than before. The circle began to spin at a fantastic speed while a shrill, whistling noise pierced the children's ears. The jewelled key seemed to melt into a pool of fire. It flickered and flowed until it slowly changed into a circle of light similar to the one now spinning so swiftly above the children.

The two circles moved towards each other, slowly at first, then faster and faster until they touched. With a shower of liquid fire they became one great spinning wheel which silently floated downwards, surrounding the children in a colourful, sparkling mist through which they could no longer see their surroundings.

"Come here, Twitch. Quickly," Charlotte called anxiously.

Brighter and brighter the light sparkled. The whistling noise started again, so loud and shrill that they all had to cover their ears, for their heads felt as if they would burst.

With their hands over their ears and their eyes tightly closed, Jeremy and Charlotte waited for what felt like a long time. All at once the sound stopped and the lights were gone.

Again, in that sudden silence there could be heard the sound of a far-off bell. Once, twice and now a third time it sounded. Louder than ever before. Then the silence returned.

When the children opened their eyes, a fresh breeze was blowing on their faces. They were now in a wide, grassy garden, deep within the castle walls, which stretched in every direction around them. As they looked about, they could clearly see the way ahead, for there was only the one path. It led straight through the carpets of flowers, towards a grey, stone building with small, narrow windows and high turrets along the walls.

"It's just like a toy castle," said Jeremy. "It even has a small moat around it!"

"Not quite a toy," Charlotte replied. "It's big enough for us to get into. And there's even a bridge over the moat!"

"And I can see a door," Twitch purred smugly. "A proper door this time. Not a hole in the ground, or half a rainbow."

Charlotte and Jeremy laughed. The three travellers walked through the flowers to the edge of the moat and looked across the bridge towards the door.

"What an odd door," Charlotte said.

The door was made from some curious material. It seemed to

move and shift like smoke, and it was crossed, from side to side, and from top to bottom by black, metal-like bands, one moment shining and the next moment dull. There was a low, humming noise that filled the air with a kind of music.

"It sounds like the red and blue spinning-top I used to play with on the grass, by the Fountain of Happiness," Jeremy said.

"I remember it," Charlotte added.

Without hesitation, the children stepped onto the bridge, stopping to lean over the side and look at the white pebbles which gleamed through the clear water.

"It's all too calm and peaceful to be true," said Charlotte. Her eyes searched in all directions as they moved forward the last few steps that brought them within an arm's length of the door.

"So far, so good," said Jeremy.

No strange sights had scared them and no dreadful creatures had appeared to attack them. All remained peaceful, with only the humming noise, like a hundred bees, filling the air. There were now only four keys to choose from, and the children argued as to which might be the right one. Even Twitch had his own ideas.

At last Charlotte said firmly, "We can't go on like this all day. We'll have to test each key in turn, just as we did at the last door."

"Maybe," replied Jeremy, unhappily. "But they look so fragile – I'm sure they'd break if we were unlucky."

"They won't break," said Charlotte.

"Suppose that happened," Jeremy continued. "Suppose we put the wrong key in, and it breaks. We'd be trapped here, no way to get back, and no way forward. Everything we've done would be ruined."

"You're right," said Charlotte.

But Twitch had had enough of this. "What a couple of miseries! There will be no question of any key breaking if you are careful. I don't know what's got into you both. Anyway, don't you think we should find a keyhole first? You won't get anywhere without one. Perhaps when you *do* see it, you may discover some kind of clue which will point to the correct key."

It was the longest speech that Twitch had ever made. The children were most surprised, and they realised just how sensible his words were.

"Let's look for the keyhole," Charlotte said. "It must be hidden."

No matter how they all hunted, the strange, shifting greyness of the door prevented them from seeing its surface with any clearness.

"I give up," Jeremy said in puzzled annoyance.

"Come on! Think!" Charlotte said. "It's a door, and we have the key to open it," she continued. "So it must have a keyhole."

"But where?"

Again they all stood staring.

"Wait," said Jeremy. "There's a tiny part of the door here that does not swirl about as much as the rest."

Charlotte looked and said, "You're right."

"Could that be where the keyhole is hidden?" Jeremy asked.

Charlotte bent over as close as possible. The small patch had a more silvery colour than the rest, and was hard to see properly. "There is something silver shining through," she whispered. "Let's try the keys, very gently."

As she lifted her hand towards the door, a faint fragrance surrounded her, like roses and lavender. Suddenly it became so strong that, for a moment she felt faint, and then it was gone. She found that she was unable to move, not even a finger. Her feet were as if fixed to the ground, and her arm remained stretched immovably in front of her. All she could do was to move her head. Turning it sideways she could see that Jeremy was in the same trouble as herself.

"Charlotte," he said in a scared voice, "I'm stuck. I can't move my hands or feet."

"Nor can I," groaned Charlotte. "It must have been that perfume. Did you smell it too?"

"I did," said Jeremy. "And it was just like the garden outside, you know, roses and, er, things. I can't remember the names of flowers."

Charlotte struggled hard to move. "Perhaps the spell from the perfume will wear off soon," she said hopefully.

"But sometimes the Wizard's spells can last for hundreds of years," said a pessimistic Jeremy.

Just then Charlotte felt a slight touch on her shoulder. Somehow, Twitch had jumped up, unaffected by the perfume. Maybe because he was a cat?

He tugged at the haversack until it slipped down to the ground, the keys clinking together inside.

He then opened the bag, took the keys out and started to unwrap them.

"What are you doing?" Charlotte called out. "Leave the keys alone. Please, Twitch."

Twitch took no notice. He was too intent in what he was doing. Soon the keys were laying on the ground.

"Wait," Twitch said. The cat then took the Cloak of Invisibility in his teeth and was trotting away, back towards the bridge.

At this point Twitch had moved so far behind the children that they could no longer see what he was doing. Then they heard him padding back. Now there was another sound, over and above the soft noise of his paws. It was a wet, slithering kind of noise which, try as she might, she could not recognise.

Charlotte was terrified. "It sounds like a snake," she said. Suddenly, something soft and wet covered her face, and she shrieked loudly. "Help!"

"What's happened?" Jeremy cried out.

Water dripped and ran down Charlotte's neck and shoulders, and she almost fainted with fright. Then, dimly, she was aware that Twitch was speaking to her.

"Sorry. Sorry. I'm so sorry to have scared you so much. Don't worry. It's only the cloak."

As the cold moat-water freshened her face and arms, all traces of the perfume were washed away. The spell was broken. To her joy, Charlotte found that she could move again.

"You're wonderful, Twitch," she said. But the cat was already on his way back to the moat to soak the cloak again. In just a few minutes it was Jeremy's turn to have the cold, wet cloak thrown over his head. The icy-cold water trickled down his face and inside his shirt. It was horrible and uncomfortable, but the spell was gone.

"Thanks," said Jeremy.

"Meow! It was nothing. Any cat would have done the same."

Jeremy was just telling Twitch how clever he was when Charlotte said sharply, "Hush! Look!" She pointed towards the cloak where it lay, soaking wet upon the ground. Before the children's eyes its wonderful blue and silver colours faded, first to a dull black, and then to a flat drab grey. A small, thin spark appeared, running up and down the material. In an instance the cloak shimmered, blurred and vanished. All that remained was a greenish stain on the ground. A second later even that had gone.

"It wasn't just the water," breathed Charlotte in wonder. "It was the magic within the cloak itself. It helped us that one last time."

It was like losing an old friend, and the children felt quite sad as they turned back to the door. This time they knew what to expect. They had already soaked their handkerchiefs in the waters of the moat. With them placed across their faces they were protected when the magic perfume filled the air once more.

Charlotte took the four remaining keys in her hand as she gazed at the weird door. The silvery colour still reflected through the strange patterns. It was for that reason she first tried the silver key. Holding her breath she reached towards the keyhole, Jeremy closed his eyes and crossed his fingers, whilst Twitch hunched his back and fluffed his tail in anxiety.

There was a tiny noise and then silence. No one made a sound. After a minute or two Jeremy opened his eyes to see what was happening. Then he too held his breath.

Charlotte's first choice had proven to be right. The misty shapes had cleared from the door, leaving it a pure, gleaming silver. A small keyhole was clear to be seen. The silver key fitted exactly and clicked quietly into place. The door shivered and shook for a second. The silver flowed and twisted, and seemed to turn into a whirlpool of light which swiftly drained away until there was nothing.

In front of the children appeared a shining slide. It led downwards into a deep pit, ringed with flame.

"Let's go," said Charlotte, leaping onto the slide.

The bell rang out again. Four deafening peals. Four doors successfully passed. As the last echoes of the bell rang in the children's ears, they hurtled down the slide, slipping from side to side, now on their backs, now on their fronts, until, with hardly a bump, they reached the bottom.

THE FINAL DANGERS

Down, down, down . . . It had been a long ride and now everything was silent. Although flames were rising and falling and flickering all around, the children felt no heat. Smoke floated up and over their heads in weird shapes, yet there was no smell – and none of the choking fumes of Fire World.

"I wonder where the flames come from," Charlotte said.

"They seem to pop up from the rocks," Jeremy replied.

Exactly in the way they seemed to appear from nowhere, so they vanished, only to reappear somewhere else.

Twitch was fascinated, chasing the flames, trying to catch them. He never succeeded even in getting close before they popped out, and then popped in again, just a couple of whiskers away.

This began to set Charlotte wondering. "Surely if they were only ordinary flames," she said, "Twitch would've been able to jump on one of them by now?"

"He'd have burn his paws," Jeremy added. "And then he'd have been moaning and groaning for the next three days."

"Be quiet," Charlotte said. She knelt down to look closer, putting the haversack on the ground beside her and saw that the flames were not ordinary flames at all.

"Look," she said, "they're tiny living creatures."

Kneeling beside her, Jeremy whispered in a slightly frightened voice, "They look like little goblins. Look at them, hopping into the air from nowhere, with sparks flying from their fingers. Hey! Look at those small flames burning from their hats. Oh! don't they look so ugly and bad tempered."

Charlotte was still peering closely, her forehead wrinkled into a frown. "I know what they remind me of," she answered slowly, as she leaned forward again. "They're like little candles. Goblin candles."

"Charlotte! Quickly, Charlotte!" cried Jeremy.

Charlotte jumped round to see what was the matter. She saw that the haversack was surrounded by hundreds of the goblin candles, and as both she and Jeremy tried to grasp it, it started to move. Both children flung themselves towards it in a desperate attempt to seize hold of the strap. But it was too late. As their clutching fingers were within an inch of success, their precious haversack vanished.

"The keys!" Jeremy cried. "They've gone!"

Wildly he charged about, looking everywhere for the haversack.

"What a foolish thing to do," Charlotte said. "Leaving the haversack unguarded. And out of sight behind my back too!"

"Stop being so miserable," Jeremy said. "That won't help us at all. There must be some way of making these creatures bring the haversack back."

Around them, unnoticed, a difference was taking place in the way the flames came and went. In their disappointment it was some time before the children noticed what was happening. Even then, for a while they did not understand the meaning of what they saw. The flames, instead of appearing in every part of the giant cave were now mainly clustered around one corner, and Charlotte peered hard in that direction, nudging Jeremy with her elbow.

"Look at that corner," she said. "All the golden flames are gathering closer and closer together."

"Let's go there," said Jeremy.

They tip-toed to the corner. Standing quietly in the shadows, they saw that a strange kind of activity was now taking place. Most of the flames were bobbing and bowing around one central flame of quite a different colour, much bigger and brighter than the others. The whole time its flickering light stopped, the smaller flames all around commenced the rapid flickering, until they stopped, too. Then the large one began to flash again.

"It must be a code," Jeremy said. "It must be the way the goblins speak to one another."

"The big light must be the leader, some kind of King," Charlotte added. "An important meeting must be taking place. Look how excited they all are."

Indeed, it was plain that something had made the goblins very lively. They were whirling and twisting about in a mad dance, flying rapidly up and down. All the time their flames flashed and glowed like fireworks. In the middle of all this, Jeremy suddenly had the answer.

"Its the haversack!" he shouted to Charlotte. "That's what it's all about. They think they're so clever to have stolen it from us."

"I must find a way to deal with these thieves," said Charlotte angrily. "I know, I have an idea how we can make them give the haversack back. It might be dangerous, but if it works it'll be worth the risk!"

Dangerous or not, Jeremy was willing to take the chance, and so he listened eagerly as Charlotte continued.

"The most important thing," she warned him, "is to do exactly what I tell you – and keep close to me the whole time. You too Twitch."

They all started to creep towards the goblins, where the meeting seemed to be getting wilder and wilder every moment. Closer and closer – they were now so near that they could almost touch the dancing flames, and still they had not been seen. The small creatures were so excited that, even if they had caught sight of the children, they took no notice. When Charlotte suddenly sprang forward they were completely taken by surprise. Before any of them realised what was happening, Charlotte had their king firmly grasped in her hands.

The creature almost went mad with rage. Its coloured flames flashed and glowed scarlet with anger. Surprisingly, it was cold, like ice, to the touch. Soon Charlotte's fingers were stiff and numb from its icy body. Immediately she seized hold of it, the rest of the goblins swarmed towards her. She was soon surrounded by hundreds and hundreds of the weird, flickering flames. About her feet, and dancing furiously around her head, they crowded in ever-increasing numbers, raging over the way she had captured their king. But, try as they might, dashing and flaring close to her face and arms, they could do nothing to harm her.

Charlotte walked across to the place from where the haversack had been stolen. The crowds of goblins followed, their angry flashing becoming even brighter as they found that there was nothing they could do to hurt her. Round and round the children's heads they whirled, getting caught in their hair, fastening on their clothes and clustering all over their arms and legs. Still the children remained unharmed. All they could feel was the coldness of the little creatures' bodies.

Charlotte looked to see how Twitch was managing, and smiled. He did look so funny for his fur was completely covered by the Goblin Lights, and his tail, sticking up straight behind him was lit up like a Christmas tree. His eyes were burning green with annoyance, and he shivered now and then from the cold. He kept pawing at his whiskers, pushing the lights away. But as fast as some where removed, others came to take their place and his face was outlined in fire.

Taking her eyes away from this funny sight, Charlotte turned her attention back to the goblin king, who she still held firmly in her hands. Kneeling down on the floor she waved the goblin king over the empty space where the haversack had been. There was an immediate response. As her hand rapidly swished through the air, the creature she was holding began to grow dimmer. Had she imagined it? Try again! This time Charlotte moved her hand faster, and faster still. There was no doubt about it, the goblin king was turning pale with fright at this terrible rushing through the air, so close to the ground.

Over and over again Charlotte dashed the goblin king around the place from where the haversack had been stolen. Just when she thought that it was all of no use after all, the creature suddenly blazed with light, flashing on and off so quickly that Charlotte could hardly bear to look at it. As quickly as it had started, it stopped and in the darkness that followed the children could hardly see a thing. Gradually their eyes became used to the dimness. All the other creatures were clustered together on the ground, and their tightly-packed bodies exactly outlined an empty space – exactly the same size and shape as the missing haversack.

Jeremy looked at Charlotte, giving a nod, and Charlotte smiled a reply. Then when every goblin became still, and all the flickering had stopped, the lights began to change colour. First a pale yellow, they faded into green, shimmered into an electric blue, and then, with a great burst of brilliant purple, they all disappeared. Once more the children's eyes were so dazzled that for a moment or two they could not see a thing.

They finally opened their eyes and looked around the great cave. All the golden flames had gone. The cave was empty and still. The shining silver slide down which they had entered had gone. The rocky floor was bare. But no, not quite bare, for there, exactly where the goblins had gathered, was the haversack.

Jeremy jumped to his feet and rushed to pick it up. Charlotte tore it open in frantic haste. "Are the keys still here?" she asked.

They both heard a "clink" and sighed with relief. Charlotte placed the four keys on the ground.

At last Jeremy turned his eyes away from the keys, and then he gave a laugh. "Hey, Charlotte," he said, "you're still holding the goblin king."

"Yes, I know," she replied. "I had no intention of letting him go until I knew that the keys were safe, but we have no use for him now."

Carefully she put the little creature down. For a moment he hovered, just above the ground as if not really believing he was now free. Then, again there came the blinding, purple flash, and he was gone. Yet again the darkness of the cave made everything hard to see.

As Charlotte stood there, the comforting weight of the haversack on her shoulder, she saw Twitch pad curiously over to the place where the goblin king had disappeared. Then, to her surprise, his tail shot straight upwards, and his whiskers bristled stiffly outwards. His head turned towards the children and his eyes were shining with pride. Then he opened his mouth, but no sound came out. He opened it again but only a faint half-meow resulted.

"What is it, Twitch?" asked Jeremy.

Twitch pointed downwards with his paw. The children realised that there was something he wanted them to see. Quickly they moved across towards him, but in the poor light they could, at first, see nothing of interest. Jeremy kneeled down. Now he could see the floor more clearly, *now* he could see what had agitated Twitch so much.

"Charlotte, look!" He spoke in such an odd voice that Charlotte looked up sharply and then dropped to her knees beside him.

Then she saw it too: a round, glassy-looking door set into the rocky floor of the cave. Charlotte ran her hands over its surface. It felt warm and soft to the touch. In the exact middle, next to a small keyhole was a wooden door-knob.

"Try the glass key," Jeremy suggested.

She did. The key slid into place, the lock clicked and, as she pulled at the wooden door-knob, the door opened easily and lightly on well-oiled hinges.

From another world, it seemed, came five thundering "Clangs" as the mysterious bell boomed again. Its great sound made the floor tremble beneath their feet.

As the last sound of the bell faded away, a silver ball floated through the open door. It seemed delicate and small to the children, who gazed at it in surprise, and from it came a tinkling sound which filled their ears with music. Charlotte turned, to make sure that Twitch was still with them. When she looked back at the silver ball it had grown larger. In a twinkling of an eye, the ball became huge, with its top way above the children's heads, and its sides reaching out in all directions.

"It must completely fill this place, wherever we are," said Charlotte. But when she looked around, she saw there was nothing to be filled. All the walls and the roof had gone and the silver ball now seemed to be the entire world.

The ball started to move, slowly turning round and round. The children could see their reflections in its gleaming sides, strangely shaped because the ball was so curved. It was Twitch who moved first, stalking off with his tail in the air. He looked very strong and brave as he padded around.

Then, with the speed of lightning disaster struck.

There was a horrible scream, and a black tube, like an elephant's trunk shot out from the side of the silver ball. On the end of the tube was a large mouth-like sucker as big as a dinner plate. In a flash the sucker clamped on the side of poor Twitch. With a great screeching

183

"Meow", his tail twisting, his eyes flashing, Twitch was drawn towards the silver ball. His claws scratched uselessly against the steel-hard sucker that had captured him. A square door opened in the side of the ball. With a last despairing wail, Twitch had gone. As he disappeared inside, there was a "click", and the door was gone too.

The great ball continued to turn slowly round and round as if nothing had happened. Neither of the children were able to make a sound.

Then another strange thing started to happen: the ball was growing smaller. Soon it was down to head high. Then the next moment only the size of a football, then no larger than a tennis ball.

"It'll vanish completely, with poor Twitch inside," cried Charlotte Even as she cried out, quick as a flash, Jeremy reached out and snatched it from the air. At once the ball stopped turning and it stopped shrinking. There it lay, in Jeremy's hand, glittering and shining.

"Twitch's trapped in there," said Charlotte.

"Maybe we could open it and get him out," said Jeremy.

"Even if we could open it, what would we find?" asked Charlotte. "Twitch must've grown smaller too. But now he's probably no bigger than a beetle."

"We'd have to keep him in a matchbox," said Jeremy.

"It isn't funny," said Charlotte.

As they talked, the silver ball was changing again. Its silvery shine was fading away, like a light gradually going out. As they watched in alarm the bright silver took on a greyish appearance and dull-black spots began to speckle its surface.

A faint tinkling noise began to sound. It was a strange, musical noise, fading up and down as though carried on the wind. The children listened carefully, for there was something about it that seemed very important. Charlotte closed her eyes and listened.

Watching the look on her face, Jeremy was puzzled. "Hey, Charlotte!" he said.

Charlotte sat up and opened her eyes. "Sh! Listen!" was all she said. She leaned back and closed her eyes again.

Jeremy did what he was told. Closing his eyes, he listened to the tinkling music. It was not long before both children heard the words which were echoing through their minds. How these words were formed, the children could not say.

"Put me down! Put me down!" it cried. "The heat is destroying me. Please put me down!"

Charlotte turned to Jeremy in surprise. "What can it mean?" she wondered. "What heat is it talking about?"

The black speckles now covered nearly all of the silver ball, and the faint tinkling music sounded again. "Please put me down. I cannot stand heat. I am dying."

The voice faded away to nothing, and the ball was now almost completely dark. Although they waited, the children did not hear the music again.

"It's the heat of your hand!" Charlotte shouted. "Quickly! Put the ball down before it's completely dead."

Jeremy nearly dropped it in his haste. In a second he had gently placed the ball on the ground, near to his feet.

"Whether it dies or not Jeremy," warned Charlotte, "if it looks as though it is getting smaller again, snatch it up."

But her warning was not needed. The little ball did not alter in size. In fact, for a moment no change of any kind took place, and the children wondered if they had been too late. Charlotte knelt down beside it, to see more closely, and she was glad to see that, after a minute or two, a few of the black spots began to fade.

"I think it's recovering," she whispered.

Both children were kneeling within a few inches of the little ball. Holding their breaths, they saw it slowly change from black to grey, and from grey to silver until it was, once more, the shining globe they had first seen. Suddenly the air was filled with joyful, tinkling music.

The children listened with all their attention, but there were no more words. After some time the ball once again began to turn very, very slowly.

"It is growing larger!" Charlotte said.

First, barely the size of an apple, it was soon the size of a pumpkin. Soon it was the same height as Charlotte, suddenly the size of a car, then a house. In the twinkling of an eye it was so immense that the children could see neither the top, nor the sides as they curved away into the distance.

Slowly the ball ceased to turn and the music faded away. "We must get in and find Twitch," Charlotte said. "We must search every inch of the side of the ball and find a door."

"We mustn't keep together," Jeremy said. "If another of those arms, with its horrible sucker shoots out, it must not catch both of us."

Charlotte nodded as she replied. "But not so far apart that we can't see each other, Jeremy. Or we won't know if anything happened."

The children walked on and on round the curving, shining sides, which seemed to extend in front and behind them forever.

They had no idea how long they walked round and round the ball. They still couldn't find any door.

Jeremy stopped suddenly and said, "Wait!"

"What is it?" called Charlotte as she ran to his side.

Set against the side of the silver ball was a small ladder, and at the top of the ladder was a door. It was shaped like a triangle and seemed barely large enough for anyone to enter. It was silver, just like the giant ball, and it was tightly shut. No handle could be seen or any mark on its shiny surface.

"Let's get up the ladder," Jeremy said, and started climbing.

Charlotte followed. "I can see a small, red jewel glowing and shining. I know what key we need."

Jeremy watched silently as Charlotte took the red, jewelled key from the haversack and passed it on to him. He placed the key against the jewel which shone so brightly in the door. Instantly, the two flashing jewels melted together and became one huge blaze of fire which spread until it covered the whole door. Then, in a flash, the fire disappeared.

The great bell rang its story of success with six deafening peals, then sounded outwards and outwards in a hundred echoes.

Jeremy reached out with a trembling hand to push the door. Gently at first, then harder. But the door did not move an inch. Again he pushed, harder still, then with all his strength, but still the door would not open.

"Charlotte," he called in a frightened voice, "I can't move it. Help me push."

Together, the children heaved, and strained, and pushed. Although they tried again and again, until they were red in the face, and puffing for breath, they could not move the door.

"It must surely have been the right key," said Charlotte, puzzled.

"And the bell has sounded," added Jeremy. "What could be wrong?"

"We must keep trying," Charlotte said.

Again they heaved, and pushed, and strained, and gasped until suddenly Jeremy stopped. Putting his hands over his face, he started to laugh whilst Charlotte stood and looked at him in amazement.

"Oh Charlotte!" he gasped through his fit of giggles. "We are idiots. Look! There are no hinges. The door doesn't swing open – it slides."

He stood to the side, and with the lightest of touches with his finger-tips the door slid softly and noiselessly out of sight.

Quietly they stepped through the narrow entrance, and as they did so, Twitch strolled across to meet them."

"What happened to you Twitch? Are you alright?"

"Course I am," replied the cat. "I'm pretty tough, you know."

They turned their attention to their new surroundings. Not that there was anything special to see. A small path led across a field of daisy-speckled grass, towards a little cottage. Where the path ended was a white-painted, plain-looking back door.

"It looks so peaceful," said Jeremy. "Let's walk down the path and open the cottage door."

Charlotte turned to whisper to Jeremy, "It's not going to be as easy as it looks. There has to be something dangerously wrong along the way. The Wizard's not going to let us win so easily. Charlotte moved towards the start of the path and knelt down to look closely.

"Well," she said, "they look like ordinary stones to me! Some are big, some are small, just like they are in all paths."

"There doesn't seem to be anywhere for any terrible monster to hide," said Jeremy.

Charlotte took one step forward. Now she was on the path. Another step, then another, but nothing happened. The sky remained blue, and the birds were still singing. She looked down at the stony path. It had not changed, and still looked very ordinary.

Slowly, one step at a time, the children moved towards the cottage door. Five, ten, twenty paces. With still nothing happening to harm them, the children were feeling braver.

Halfway along the path, just as Charlotte turned to smile at Jeremy, the most terrible things started to happen.

Before they had started off along the pathway Charlotte had noticed that a great grey stone lay right across it. Now, as they came close to this stone, the entire pathway seemed to come alive, twisting and bending beneath their feet, wriggling and turning like a giant snake. The children screamed in deadly fear as they tried to keep upright, finding themselves being jolted backwards and forwards as the snake path rippled underneath them. Behind them, still twisting and grinding in every direction, the path began to rise into the air and soon they were desperately trying to keep their balance on a steep slope.

Up and up, steeper and steeper rose the path, until its shaking, twisting movement started to force the children to stagger towards the great grey stone which still remained solidly blocking the way ahead. It was the only direction for them to run. But, as the children fled down the snaking path towards it, they skidded, shrieking to a stop. They now saw that it was really some kind of terrible stone-shaped creature. The entire surface of it had changed into a giant, red mouth with jagged, yellow teeth and, most horrible of all, there was a thick, black tongue flickering in and out and around, seeking to sweep them all into its sticky, tunnel-like throat.

"Try not to move!" Charlotte screamed, and the children leaned backwards, digging their heels in, as the path became even steeper, in its attempts to force them towards the rock-mouth. In absolute terror, Charlotte realised that it was impossible not to move. Slipping and sliding they found themselves slowly forced towards that awful, gaping throat. By now the path behind them was like a wall, reaching straight upwards into the sky. The children were pushed onwards, onwards, until only a few feet separated them from that final horror.

"There's only one chance," Charlotte said, as she moved faster than she had ever done before.

"What?" cried Jeremy.

Thrusting Twitch into Jeremy's shaking arms, Charlotte took the last key from the haversack and placed it safely in her pocket. Then, with all her strength, she hurled the haversack directly into the centre of the evil, gaping mouth now almost at her feet.

As the haversack landed on the thick, ugly tongue, the teeth closed greedily, and the lips of purple-grey stone twisted into every kind of horrible shape as the mouth started to tear and chew. Grind! Grind! Gulp! The harder the teeth tore at the haversack the more they became entangled in its hard, thick material.

It was not long before the giant mouth grew tired of this. Then it made its fatal mistake. Twisting and stretching ,the monster tried to swallow its difficult and tasteless meal, the mouth opening like a terrible cavern. The torn and tangled remains of the haversack stuck hard in its throat, and the more the yellow teeth crashed together, and the more the black, leathery tongue lashed about, the harder the haversack stuck.

The mouth choked and gulped in frantic attempts to clear the blockage from its throat. The path thrashed about and shook like an earthquake, and the children were tossed to the ground, rolling from one side to the other, quite unable to protect themselves from the hard stones which were cutting and bruising their arms and legs.

Gradually, everything became quiet once more. Dazed, frightened and covered with dust, the children realised that at last the path was still again. There was a deep silence broken only by the singing of a small bird, high in the blue sky. For a while the children did not dare to move.

Stones and rocks had been thrown all over the place, and the little winding path, which had been so smooth and tidy, was now jagged and full of holes. The huge mouth of the path monster was open, and still and already the sun was shrivelling up the great, black tongue which hung down sideways. The remains of the haversack were still firmly stuck, half-way down the throat.

"There's the last door," Charlotte said, as she ran towards the cottage." She was holding the golden key firmly in her hand. She slowly placed the key in the lock. Still with her hand resting on the key she looked at Jeremy and Twitch.

"Now?" she asked with a smile.

"Yes," whispered Jeremy.

"Meow," said Twitch, standing up to rub his head on Charlotte's knee.

So, Charlotte moved her hand. The key turned, and the final door began to swing open. So many thoughts passed through the children's minds as they saw it slowly move. What would they find when they stepped through? Did the Wizard intend to stop them somehow, here at the very end? Most of all, were their parents *really* here?

One step. Two steps. The children now stood in the doorway itself. Then, on the third step a deafening mind-filling, almost frightening thunder of bells rang out. One! Two! Three! Four! Five! Six! Seven! The children put their hands over their ears for the noise was so great.

In just a short moment, the echoes of the great bells stopped. A quietness fell, such as the children had never known. There was a darkness so complete that they felt they could hardly breathe. Through the darkness and the quietness a voice spoke softly.

"You have won through the greatest dangers ever known. You have defeated the worst of my spells. You have shown me what happiness and love means, and because of all that, I no longer need to steal the Fountain of Happiness. Your bravery and courage have won for you the return of all you desire. I am the Wizard of every world in which you have fought my spells. Although I have used my darkest enchantments, you have beaten me. Now is the time for your reward. Step on through the door. I promise that I shall never harm you, or any other creature again. Good-bye."

A gentle breeze blew from the darkness.

"Let's go," Charlotte said to Jeremy. "Come on, Twitch."

There was soft grass beneath their feet. The glowing sun brightened the sky. In front of them, water glittered and sparkled, making a beautiful rainbow. There, where the rainbow ended, two

190

people sat up and looked around, as if still in a dream.

"Mummy, Daddy," the children cried. Half running, half rolling down the sloping grass, they threw themselves into their parent's open arms. Soon all four were sitting beside the magic fountain, so glad to be together again that, at first, they could hardly speak a word.

It was much later that day that the children learned how their parents had been kept locked in that dark and dismal dungeon, wondering if they would ever see their children again. They heard, too, how their parents had been awoken by the sound of a great bell, and how this bell had rung again and again, first striking once, then twice, then more and more, until finally it rang seven times. Then, for some strange reason the children's parents had fallen into a deep sleep. When they awoke they were here, by the Fountain of Happiness. And the first thing they saw was the children running towards them.

The parents wanted to know everything that had happened. So, beside the wonderful fountain, back in their own home at last, as the days and weeks passed, Jeremy and Charlotte told of their long trail of danger and adventure. Many times the story filled their parents with fear over the dreadful things that could have happened to the children.

Months passed. Living in their own cottage with their parents and sleeping in their own beds, and playing in the sun by the Fountain of Happiness, their search for the Seven Keys seemed to be like a half-forgotten dream.

What happened to Twitch? He stayed with Jeremy and Charlotte. Although he never spoke again, sometimes he would slowly wink one golden-green eye, and give a special "purr-meow", and Charlotte would remember . . .